Praise for
I CAN SEE IN THE DARK

"Fossum descends deep into the alienated mind of Riktor to create an exquisitely Poe-ish novel of psychological suspense." — *More*

"The queen of Norwegian crime fiction, the prolific and brilliant Fossum, has riddled the quaint countryside north of Oslo with imagined crimes . . . In Fossum's literary thrillers, the crime is almost incidental to a deeper moral crisis: Her killers aren't madmen but ordinary people driven to monstrous acts." — *Men's Journal*

"A taut, well-paced book. Chilling." — *Dallas Morning News*

"Fossum vividly unpacks the mind of a troubled individual in this haunting psychological thriller . . . Compelling — if unsettling — character study for fans of psychological suspense."
— *Library Journal*

"Readers who can handle the darkest tales will be rewarded by Fossum's streamlined, thoughtfully constructed story." — *Booklist*

"[A] first-rate novel of suspense . . . [A] clever and compelling standalone." — *Publishers Weekly,* starred review

"A chilling portrait of a dead-eyed devil." — *Kirkus Reviews*

I CAN SEE IN THE DARK

Also by Karin Fossum

I Can See in the Dark

the Dark

Karin Fossum

Translated from the Norwegian
by James Anderson

Mariner Books
Houghton Mifflin Harcourt
BOSTON • NEW YORK

First Mariner Books edition 2015

Copyright © 2011 by Karin Fossum

English translation copyright © 2013 by James Anderson

First published with the title *Jeg kan se i mørket* in 2011
by Cappelen Damm AS, Oslo

First published in Great Britain in 2013 by Harvill Secker

For information about permission to reproduce selections from this book,
write to Permissions, Houghton Mifflin Harcourt Publishing Company,
215 Park Avenue South, New York, New York 10003.

www.hmhco.com

Library of Congress Cataloging-in-Publication Data
Fossum, Karin, date.
[Jeg kan se i mørket. English]
I can see in the dark / Karin Fossum ; translated from
the Norwegian by James Anderson.
pages cm
ISBN 978-0-544-11442-5
ISBN 978-0-544-48398-9 (pbk.)
I. Title.
PT8951.16.O735J4413 2014
839.823'8—dc23
2014002823

Book design by Brian Moore

Printed in the United States of America
DOC 10 9 8 7 6 5 4 3 2 1

I CAN SEE IN THE DARK

1

THERE'S NOTHING BEAUTIFUL about her, and she has no control. She can't control her eyes, which dart around or roll up into her head, so that only the glistening whites are visible. Or her body, which does what it likes. Her skin is stretched tight over her joints, the veins giving her a greenish pallor, and she's as thin as a small bird. Children shouldn't look like this. Children should be plump, pink and warm, soft as rubber, and full of sparkling life. I assume her condition was caused by an injury during birth.

She's about nine or ten and confined to a wheelchair.

Her mother calls her Miranda, a stupid name. Well, in my opinion anyway. Her hair is very fine and fair, and gathered in a knot at the top of her head. Her hands move around restlessly—white, claw-like hands that are incapable of doing anything. You'd think she was attached to an electric current. That someone was switching it on and off, sending shocks through her delicate body. I get very twitchy watching little Miranda. Worn out by all these spasms—this constant agitation—I feel like screaming. If she really were powered by electricity, I'd want to pull the plug. I'd enjoy seeing her jerking body relax.

Miranda can't speak. She only makes noises and unintelligible exclamations; I can't understand any of it, even though I've had plenty of experience with all sorts of helplessness. I've worked in nursing homes for more than seventeen years.

I often see Miranda here, because they come to the park by Lake Mester every day without fail. Like me, they follow a routine; they need something to cling to, a groove that feels safe. The young mother takes care of the little thing; she hasn't any choice. One heady moment with a man has turned into a lifelong burden. If anyone else comes into the park, she glances up quickly, but without any anticipation of adventure. What kind of man would approach this pair and willingly take on these problems, the ever-present child, ceaselessly gesticulating and yammering all day long?

Carrying the child around.

Wheeling the child around.

Never watching her run across the floor.

I go to the park at various times of the day because I work shifts, and I'm often free when others are at work. I've been coming here a long time, and I take note of all the other people who enjoy sitting on the benches admiring the fountain and its splashing water. The sound of the water has a strangely analgesic effect. For those of us who live with pain. I don't sleep much, and the nights are long and agonizing. I try to maintain my grasp of reality; I don't think people notice anything peculiar about me, either here in the park or where I work at Løkka Nursing Home. My manner is calm and friendly, and I do what I'm told; I simply mimic the others who stay within the norm. It's easy. I talk like them, laugh like them, tell funny stories. But with all the feeble elderly people under my care, things often slide out of control. Especially for those who can't speak or haven't the strength to complain.

Maybe they think: I don't want to live, but I don't want to die. Life becomes so impossible as it nears its end. They just lie there clutching at a duvet, sightless, voiceless, and unable to hear. Without any desire for the dregs of life, and full of fear for death.

I like sitting in the park and watching the people. They look so vulnerable on the green benches in the sun, with their eyes fixed on the lovely fountain. Three dolphins, each spouting a jet of water from its mouth. The park is small and pretty, quite intimate in its way, but the benches are hard and have armrests of cast iron. I almost envy Miranda her wheelchair and the pillow at her back. And the rug over her legs in the evenings, when it gets chilly. Her mother chain-smokes. She throws the butt on the ground and immediately lights another, inhaling so hard her cheeks are sucked in. She, too, is fettered to that chair with its large wheels. But there *is* something between them, I think, as I watch them surreptitiously. A frail bond, because it's needful—they have to fulfill these roles, play this game, mother and child.

Sometimes I go to the park and find it deserted, but I love sitting there alone on my green bench. The park is my own little kingdom then, and I'm in complete control. I'm responsible for everything. I make the water tinkle, I make the flowers bloom, and if I wish, I make the birds sing. I force the wind softly through the leaves; I chase the clouds across the sky. And if I'm in a good mood, I add a butterfly or a woolly bumblebee.

I think about Miranda's mother a lot. Occasionally she glances at me, entreatingly, like a beggar.

Take me away from all these problems, the glance says. I want a different life.

That's what everyone wants, surely.

2

AT THE ENTRANCE to the park, just as you turn along a narrow, paved path, there is a beautiful sculpture. *Woman Weeping*.

I'm not well traveled, but I've never seen anything like it— never seen anything so lovely and so riveting as this sculpture. I've never seen anyone cry the way she's doing. She's on her knees; she's succumbed to it completely, weighed down with suffering and grief. Her hands hide her face, her long hair has fallen forward, and her shoulders are hunched in hopeless despair. It's heartening that an artist has got to grips with the anguish we all feel. Our sorrow about life itself and the torment of existence, braving each of its seconds and minutes, tolerating the gaze of others. There are plenty of other wonderful sculptures. Beautiful women with outstretched arms; athletic men; chubby, laughing children.

But give me *Woman Weeping*.

Give me the truth about human beings and life.

She's cast from gilded bronze, which has a lovely luster. When the sun streams through the leaf canopy, she turns warm and golden like an ember. In winter her body is as cold as ice, with its round shoulders and the narrow back, through which vertebrae protrude like marbles beneath the skin. When no one is looking, I stroke her slender body, her long legs, her slim ankles.

But my thoughts constantly return to Miranda.

She needs help with everything all the time. I often think about that—help from morning to night, every hour, around the clock. Help when she's thirty and when she's forty. At some point, her mother won't be there anymore, and who will look after her then? It's just this sort of helpless case that ends up at the nursing home where I work, that ends up at Løkka. Then they're handed over to me with all my quirks and fancies, my outbursts and attentions. Within me lurks an evil little devil who occasionally asserts himself. He's impossible to avoid, because sometimes the temptation is too great. I'd never have believed it of Riktor, people would say in all their ignorant innocence, if they knew the truth about me and the things I'm capable of. I can see right through people. I can see what's concealed in their innermost, shadowy recesses. And when it comes to evil, I can believe anything of anybody.

3

OUR WARD SISTER Anna Otterlei is an exception.

The well-being of the patients is much more than a career choice. It's her life's mission, or so it seems, and she's quite inexhaustible. She's loving, self-sacrificing, and serene. She cares and comforts, she nurses and soothes. She's constantly in their rooms, sitting on a chair by the bed, speaking softly and confidingly, stroking their cheeks with a warm hand. She finds out what they need and what they dream of, and shares the sorrows of a lifetime that will soon be at an end. She partakes in their fear of death—that final, slow descent into darkness. Personally I can't be bothered. If you extend a hand, you only receive tears and despair in return. These are doors I don't want to open; I have enough of my own as it is. I've enough of my own pounding heart, with all the whisperings in the corners. Evil tongues that know, perhaps, what I really am.

Sometimes at night, a truck drives into my bedroom; it comes roaring through the door and parks next to my bed. Its diesel engine throbs until dawn. I'm worn out by the time I finally put my feet on the floor on the other side of the bed. Silence frightens me even more, because I've lived my whole life in this din, with these voices and this noise.

But then there's my angel, Sister Anna. She's lovely, but she's also sharp, like a cake with sweet icing and a bitter little berry in the middle. She's the one I'm most cautious with. The rest of the staff on the ward aren't clever enough to see through me; they haven't the sensitivity for unraveling human riddles. And I am one such human riddle.

If only I had a woman! A woman like Sister Anna, with her beauty and her wisdom, her indomitable desire to be good. She's blonde and bosomy and beautiful, with a high, arched brow and plump cheeks, like those of a small well-nourished child. Lips as red as cherries, a neck like a swan's, eyes that seem to gaze down from on high, with the barest twinkle in them. She's about the same age as me, in her early forties. And although she's constantly looking in my direction, it's not with any desire or yearning. I have none of the qualities women dream of. But I like being near her, catching the scent and the warmth of her; she warms like a stove. She shines like a sun. She sails like a ship. Truly she's a woman after my own depraved heart.

Everyone has virtues, everyone has a talent, everyone has a right to respect. That's how we human beings like to think. But rotten individuals do exist and, I have to admit, I'm one of them: a rotten individual who in certain situations can turn spiteful, to the extent that I become almost unhinged. But I find no difficulty in aping other people, aping politeness and friendliness and kindness. It's restraining the bad impulses that's tough. I often think of the things that might happen if I really lost control, and that does happen from time to time.

But then there's Sister Anna, pretty little Anna. She is the angel in the human story. Sometimes, when she comes along the corridor, I go weak and wobbly at the knees. But the joy of kissing Anna's cherry-red lips will never be mine. I know too much about the commerce of love.

4

I LIVE AT Jordahl on the outskirts of town. I have a small red house half an hour's walk from the park by Lake Mester. It was built in 1952, with that typical end-of-war restraint: spartan, simple, and practical. Living room and kitchen, bedroom and bathroom, and that's all. Two old wrought-iron stoves that purr throughout the winter and a large covered veranda where I sit and watch the people who pass by. It's easy to maintain, with heavy furniture that has no decorative refinement. There's a forest at the back of the house, of spruce and birch. The house used to have a lovely lawn in front, but now it's completely overgrown. Occasionally, during the summer, I cut it with a scythe. I enjoy playing the Grim Reaper; I feel at home in the part.

It takes me forty minutes to walk to the nursing home at Løkka. And I walk whatever the weather, even though the bus stops at the entrance. There's something about walking; it orders the thoughts, puts them into perspective. My house is on a rise, facing west; and in the evenings the sun shines through my living-room window like a great glowing sphere. It hangs there a moment, casting a golden glow, until the rooms shimmer with heat. Then it sinks behind a stand of trees. Slowly everything turns blue.

All the shrubs and trees, and the wooded hillsides in the distance.

It's then that my head begins to seethe. Billions of tiny creatures swarm through my brain, digging tunnels and severing the essential communications I need to be able to think, reason, and plan. Good deeds and bad: it varies, I've so many irons in the fire. Normally I go to the window and stand there looking out, waiting for everything to calm down. And sometimes there really is a hush. As when someone switches off a flow of words. Then I find the silence troubling and immediately switch on the radio or television just to hear voices. Sometimes, when I'm with people, I find I'm on the verge of panic for no reason whatsoever. I assume a friendly expression so that no one will see what's happening to me, that I'm existing in chaos.

I've never mentioned any of this to a doctor. Even though we have a doctor on the ward and I could have confided in him. We are colleagues, after all. You see, I might have said to Dr. Fischer, my head begins to seethe when the sun goes down. It's like thousands of ants, like a swarm of crawling insects. There are whispers in the corners of my bedroom, and an articulated truck parks next to my bed. Its engine idles the whole night long, and I can hardly breathe for all the diesel fumes. But you don't go telling people things like that. Although he's a doctor, it would make him think, and I don't want to cause myself embarrassment.

5

I CAN SEE bushes and trees, buildings, posts, and fences. I can see them all vividly glowing and quivering, long after dark. I see the heat they emit, a sort of orange-colored energy, as if they're on fire. I once mentioned this to the school nurse when I was about ten. That I could see in the dark. She simply patted me on the cheek and then smiled sadly, the way you smile at an inquisitive child with a lively imagination. But once bitten, twice shy: I never mentioned it again. Sometimes at night, when it's impossible to sleep—when the truck has been standing at my bedside for hours and filled the entire room with exhaust fumes—I get dressed and go out and stand on the driveway. I watch the moving creatures in the landscape, everything that hides from the noise and light of day. A fox darting over the fields, a deer bounding across the road, everything pulsing with this amber light.

The living-room windows give on to the driveway and the road, while the kitchen window looks out on the forest of tall trees. This gives me a sense of living in seclusion, but I have neighbors. Just below me is Kristian Juel's house; he minds his own business and doesn't bother me much, for which I'm grateful. Next door, up the hill, is a family with young children. They do a lot of screaming and shouting and bouncing on a large trampoline, as well as chasing a small dog that barks all the time. Sometimes, on light summer nights, I hear the laughter and barking and think they sound like church bells carried on the air. At other times, they get on my nerves and I feel like screaming.

But then there's our ward sister Anna.

Elegant, warm, and radiant.

There isn't her equal anywhere.

Once, when I was a child, a classmate announced in a malicious, jeering way that I looked like a pike. It was probably because my jaw protrudes slightly and I have sharp, crooked teeth like a predatory fish. As the boy in question was somewhat overweight, I pointed out that he ought to shut up because he resembled a beached whale. That left him completely stranded, and I could tell he regretted his little sally. That's all I remember about my childhood. Almost everything else has been erased and consigned to oblivion. But I always remember the pike episode. I remember the feeling of humiliation, how my cheeks burned, and how I was almost blind with rage. I'm not much to look at; I've known that for a long time. My eyes are too close together and deep-set, with irises the color of cod liver oil. Sometimes I skulk in the bushes bordering the path that leads into the park. I just stand there and peer out at the passing pedestrians. Old people with sticks; elderly, lonely men; little girls in short, flaring skirts, tittering and gossiping, dangerous as death caps.

6

DR. FISCHER, WHO'S in charge of our ward, was once an idealist—or at least I imagine that he was—with a genuine desire to assuage the pain of others. Alleviating discomfort and despair is important to people right at the end of their lives.

Dignified and self-sacrificing, he wanted to move among the beds, making a difference. Now he has a resigned and round-shouldered look as he mooches from room to room, wearing shabby suede shoes and a downcast expression. He has worked at Løkka Nursing Home for more than twenty years, and the people he cares for only have a short time to live. It's as if the mere thought of this takes his breath away. He also possesses a very fastidious conscience. It cries out over the least little thing, as if all the misery in the world were his fault. It's often struck me that one fine day this troublesome conscience will be the death of him because such things weaken the entire organism. He has a habit of massaging his temple, as if there's something in there that's irritating him. A difficult idea, perhaps, or a painful recollection. Each time he sits down to rest, he raises his hand and begins the massage. His job is strenuous. In my mind's eye, I see a thousand hands tugging and tearing at his coat, grabbing at his hair, forcing him up against the wall.

I need help, voices cry. I must have relief, I want more, and right away!

Painkillers, sleeping pills—something that eases fear and anxiety, something that lessens grief and hopelessness. He can't get away. Perhaps he's got problems at home to wrestle with too, for all I know. A wife whom he no longer loves, children who have no respect for him. He's trapped in his world, trapped in his white coat, his pricking conscience chasing him up and down the corridors. I sense that Dr. Fischer doesn't like me. He's out to get me, I think. He'll catch me, if he has the chance; he's always waiting for an opportunity. I'm very sensitive to such things. It's something to do with energy, or lack of energy. Nothing flows between us, no warmth, no sympathy.

I keep out of his way, for he's a kind of harbinger of things to come.

I've never seen him in the park near Lake Mester.

Ten minutes' walk from the park is the Dixie Café, half hidden among a clump of birch trees, with its dark green plastic tables and chairs. Two large palm trees in blue pots stand by the door. They're artificial, of course. Perhaps the owner thinks this is an exotic touch; but there, among the birches, they simply look odd. The Dixie has a youthful clientele. They buy burgers and Coke, and loiter by the wall, nudging and jostling each other in a friendly way. I've walked there a couple of times and sat at one of the plastic tables with a Styrofoam cup of anemic coffee, watching the youngsters. They don't inhabit the same world as me. Perhaps it's more that I've been cut adrift from everyone else, as if a cord has been severed. Or the wheels of time have worn it through. I don't really understand my own situation; I don't understand this sense of always being an outsider, of not belonging, of not feeling at home in the day's routines. Forces I can't control have torn me away from other people. I like being on my own, but I want a woman. If only I had a woman!

• • •

13

At this point, I might mention that when I was a small boy, I found my father hanging from a rafter one day. His face was engorged and bluish black, and a great thick tongue stuck out from between his lips. If nothing else, it would help explain why I'm the way I am. But it's not true. My father was a decent man and he never hurt a fly. Distant and detached he certainly was, but he didn't hang himself from a rafter. He died when I was fourteen, of a massive thrombosis.

I'm sure Dr. Fischer is soft on Sister Anna and has his dark and wistful eye on her. Perhaps Sali Singh, who works in the kitchen, has too. I notice such things immediately.

There's a lot of communication between human beings that isn't expressed in words, and I'm exceedingly observant. Some people don't understand this. They concentrate on what's being said, while others, like me, become masters of the hint, the tiny signals that tell. A quick glance at Sali and I know how he's feeling, even though he may have his back to me. I look at his shoulders and notice if they're hunched. Is he standing four-square or tripping around nervously. I take in how the movement of his hands emanates from his squat body: evenly or in fits and starts, haltingly or fluently. Sali is a big man; most of his weight is around his waist. I wonder what he thinks about Norway and Norwegians, deep down in his dusky, Indian heart. Probably nothing very flattering; we're so unbearably spoiled. But he makes lovely open sandwiches, standing in his kitchen at Løkka. He's indifferent to budgets, so he just loads the bread generously with all manner of good things. How odd that must seem to a man who can hardly be a stranger to poverty. His eyes are almost black. His oily hair takes on a bluish sheen, as he stands there working beneath the fluorescent lighting.

7

EDDIE AND JANNE are often at the park.

I used to think of them as Romeo and Juliet, but that was before I knew their names. The other day they were calling to each other in the spring air, like two playful children. Look at this, Janne; no, stop messing around, Eddie; and so on in that vein. They sit close together on the bench, entwined in each other. They neck and pat and stroke, purring like cats. I've never seen anything like it. They'd eat each other, skin, hair, and all, if only they could. And they're never self-conscious, even when there are several of us sitting by the fountain. I notice that some people break into soft smiles and others turn away because they don't like it. Personally, I don't know what to think, but surely this is something private; there should be more decorum in public. And nothing about Eddie and Janne is decorous. They always bring something to eat. When they've given each other a thorough squeezing, they open a bag of buns, or a bar of chocolate. They eat the way children do, with unabashed greed. Eddie is perhaps sixteen or seventeen, Janne possibly a little younger. Both are slim and good-looking, clad in precisely the same costume of distressed jeans and gray hoodies. Both have dark hair that's identically styled: close-shaved at the sides with a comb of hair on the crown. You can hardly tell them apart.

I remember Sali saying that when he first came to Norway, he couldn't tell the difference between men and women. Everyone wears jeans, he said, and sneakers. The women cut off their hair. It is not very nice; why don't they make themselves look more beautiful? I explained that climate dictates the way we dress. Norwegian women can't go around in saris and sandals, I said. You know what the autumns and winters are like here.

Eddie and Janne will never get married, never have children, or own a house or a car; they will never experience responsibility and debt and difficult days. The bond between them is only a frail alliance, although they don't know it themselves. Sometimes a wave of sadness washes over me when I think of the impending breakup: the tears and recriminations, the bewilderment that it didn't last, the apportioning of blame. When I'm feeling generous, they put me in mind of newly opened tulips, as they sit on their bench. It's April. The thaw is here and everything melts and runs away; there's too much of everything. It's an agonizing and confusing time that chills my back as I sit on the bench in front of the fountain, while my face is gently warmed by the sun. My jacket comes off and goes on again; coltsfoot squeezes up through the snow; and crisp, wafer-thin ice decks the puddles in the morning. The asphalt is bare, so summer shoes can come out of the cupboard. But it remains deep winter in the forest, with dark and frosty nights.

I often think about the old people in their beds at Løkka. Those cavernous faces, those bony hands always groping for something to hold on to. They, who have seen and understood the most about life and how it should be lived. I know so much more now, they think; I understand things at last, but it's too late. Now the greenhorns are coming to take over, and they won't listen to us, lying here twittering like birds.

· · ·

Arnfinn comes to the park a little later in the day.

He appears on the paved path and ignores *Woman Weeping*. He takes short, tentative steps because he's frightened of falling. With an apologetic look, he seats himself on his usual bench and listens to the splashing water. His hands tremble violently much of the time. At first I thought he had Parkinson's. Then, having kept him under observation for some time, I realized that he's an alcoholic. He has periods when he doesn't drink. Often this is when his Social Security has run out—he's certainly on Social Security. But usually he has a hip flask in his pocket. Of vodka or brandy, or whatever it is he pours into himself. Clearly this flask is a sovereign remedy. After a few pulls, he slowly relaxes. His breath comes calmly and easily, his features soften, his eyes glisten. He wears an old Windbreaker and thick, stained trousers that are too short for him. He doesn't bother to tie his lace-up shoes. This is the costume he always wears whatever the time of year, and I can even picture him sleeping with his clothes on. I imagine him simply collapsing on a sofa, wearing his shoes and everything. He talks to himself a bit; he sits there mumbling unintelligibly, but he cringes if I turn my eyes in his direction. I don't know if he eats anything. His hip flask looks very refined. It speaks of a different time when perhaps he had a job, a family, and responsibilities. It could be made of silver and was possibly a fortieth or fiftieth birthday present; now he's probably sixty-something. He often has this hip flask with him. He pats his pocket to make sure it's there. His hands are like great meat-colored clubs. Presumably he's done a lot of manual work; you can see that his body is well used. His hair is gray and his face florid, as the arteries in it are blocking up. This process forces the blood to find new passages beneath the skin.

When we're sitting in the park, he sends surreptitious glances in Miranda's direction. It's hard to guess his thoughts when he sees that little cripple; she's often screaming and impossible to ignore. Sometimes she hits her mother with her fist. That's human beings for you: If we can't find the words, we fall back on the fist.

One day, when Arnfinn and I were alone in the park, he tottered off down the path without his hip flask. It lay there on the bench after he'd gone, silver and shining, but I didn't notice it until he'd vanished among the trees. I was curious and went over immediately to take a closer look. It really was a most elegant hip flask, with a screw top and a cap to drink from, and, last but not least, a neatly engraved inscription.

Here's to Arnfinn.

I unscrewed the top and held the flask to my nose. It contained a small amount of liquid that was almost odorless, so I concluded it must be vodka. I stood with the hip flask in my hand, unsure of what to do. Obviously if I left it there, someone would take it. So I put it in my inside pocket; it didn't take up much room. Naturally I'd return it at some point. I reasoned that its loss would be a large one for him, once he felt his pocket and realized it was missing. I returned to my own bench with the trophy close to my heart. I sat and admired the dolphins spouting water. This was in the morning; I was on late shift that day and wasn't due at work until two o'clock. I kept half an eye out for Arnfinn, in case he came back for his hip flask. But he didn't show up. He'd probably collapsed somewhere, on a sofa or under a bridge. You never can tell with people like that; they're past all help.

8

I'M TAKING FOOD, juice, and medicine from room to room, checking off that the old people have eaten and drunk and swallowed their tablets. But the truth is rather different. The injections go into the mattress, the food is tipped down the toilet, and ditto the drugs. Then I flush it and cover all traces. Boiled fish or mince disappears into the plumbing system, there to serve, presumably, as nutrition for rats the size of elephants. The old people wave their pale, wrinkled hands helplessly after the vanishing food. No one understands what they're saying or why they're fretting. No one at Løkka has discovered my little game. But caution is required. Some relatives enjoy creating a fuss; they watch us like hawks, making sure we're doing what we're supposed to. What *are* we supposed to be doing, I often think, especially on days when I'm feeling very tired. Are we supposed to keep them alive no matter what, by any means, for as long as possible? Even though they're on the brink of death and are unproductive and useless now, and don't even afford anyone any pleasure? I can't cope with all this helplessness, and sometimes my temper turns evil. What's the point in eating when you're almost a hundred?

Ebba often comes to the park.

She always brings something she can do with her hands—some

crocheting or knitting, a sock or a doily. There are people who can't sit quietly with their hands in their lap, and Ebba is one of them. I'd put her at close to eighty, but she's upright and strong in body, and fleet of foot. When she comes walking along the path, she often stops to admire *Woman Weeping*. She stands looking at it for a moment, her head to one side. She's always well dressed, with her hair beautifully coiffed, and her hands work industriously at her knitting or crocheting. I imagine she must have been something like a schoolteacher, a secretary, or a nursing officer in a hospital, or maybe even an accountant. But certainly a career woman. I assume she's crocheting for her children and grandchildren. Small tablecloths or long lengths destined to become bedspreads. She seems very content, both with herself and with the life she leads. She's certainly not bowed with age. She's at one with everything: with the bench she's sitting on, with the earth beneath her feet. Just occasionally, but only very rarely, she lowers her work to her lap. Then she turns her face up to the sun and closes her eyes. But, after an instant, she's off again with renewed vigor. The ball of wool on the bench beside her dances its rhythmic jig as she tugs at the yarn.

They say that Nelly Friis is blind.

That she's been blind for more than thirty years. Her relatives, a son and daughter, say so. On a rare visit to Løkka, one of her grandchildren, sitting helplessly at her bedside and wringing her hands, says that Nelly Friis is blind. Sali Singh says so too, and Dr. Fischer and Sister Anna. But I have my doubts. I've heard that supposedly blind people can actually see quite a lot of movement and deep shadow, the brightest light. In addition, they can recognize smells and can hear voices and register details and fine distinctions. They notice lots of tiny things that escape the sighted. Despite this, I often go to her room. I can't resist it. She weighs a mere forty kilos and is as fragile and gray as paper. And, in theory at least, shouldn't see that it's me, Riktor, who's entered. I bend over the bed, take hold of the delicate skin behind her ear with my long, sharp nails, and squeeze as hard as I can. The thin, dry skin is punctured. She hasn't the voice to scream nor the strength to avoid me.

I listen to check if anyone's coming along the corridor. If I'm feeling really bad, I'll tug the hair at her temples, where I know it hurts the most. She hasn't got much hair left. There are several bald patches on her scalp, and no one knows that I'm the one responsible. They think it's age and decrepitude. No one notices the red sores behind her ears; no one washes there thoroughly. There are so many who require sponging and moving and turning and massaging and a whole lot of other things; old people take a lot of work. I torture her for a good while. I notice an artery pulsing in her neck; I notice her blind, gooseberry-like eyes are filling with liquid. And I don't know how much she can see. If my face is merely a pale oval in a larger blackness without visible characteristics. If she recognizes the smell of my aftershave. It's not easy to tell. But one time, Anna and I walked into her room together, and she began to flail her hands with the little strength she had. Anna ran off to fetch Dr. Fischer. He prescribed diazepam, and after that Nelly hadn't the strength to be anxious. The torture that I inflict gives me a feeling of desperation and delight. A blissful mixture of guilt and superiority. And adrenaline, coursing hotly through my body. Pinching Nelly Friis behind the ears and giving her contusions where no one can see them causes my own pent-up frustration, my own fear and sorrow, to drain out of my body like pus from a wound.

What a wasteland this world is.

What a misfortune that we live to be so old.

This thought constantly comes into my mind.

If only I had a woman to soothe and comfort me.

Sometimes Anna follows me down the corridor in her quiet and careful way. Often, as she passes, she'll put a hand on my shoulder and give it a squeeze.

"Hi, Riktor, you all right?" she'll say, and hurry on without waiting for a reply. It's only a friendly gesture in passing, a minute distraction. But so strong is the effect of her pleasant greeting that I've known my eyes to fill with tears. I am really moved, and that doesn't happen often. Anna does things like that and they cost her nothing at all. If only she knew, I think. Nelly Friis is not the only one who's blind.

9

ONE DAY AT the beginning of April, I went out for a walk near Lake Mester. Lake Mester is a small lake, and that day its surface lay ice-bound and covered with snow in the bright, sparkling weather. All was white and smooth like a newly ironed sheet. After several days of mild conditions, and a tentative promise of spring, the cold had returned. And, as I was walking, I caught sight of a skier working his way across the fields. He came on quickly, his modern, red, skin-hugging ski-suit so visible in that overwhelming whiteness, as was the little waist pouch that gave a hop with each tug on the poles. I stood there watching him as he came down the slopes. My imagination had free rein, and each of the skier's strides seemed like a race against time. It's a question of holding age at bay, he was saying to himself perhaps; I'm on the offensive against death and decay, always one step ahead and as fit as a fiddle.

I went on a few paces as he rapidly drew nearer. He was a middle-aged man, probably in his fifties, the age at which people often begin these desperate remedies. To put it simply, he was being hounded by the demon of fitness. His arms thrust forward in almost aggressive lunges; his body seemed robust and firm in that red ski-suit. I ambled off slowly, inhaling the sharp air and keeping my eye on the red skier. There was a speed and fluidity and forcefulness about him, so it took me some time to register where he was going. He was heading toward the water, toward the lake with its covering of snow and ice. The lake in April. Can you believe it, I thought to myself, and followed him with my eyes. Naturally I assumed he'd keep to the shore. But, to my astonishment, I saw him swish out onto the ice. This daring maneuver flabbergasted me. Still I reasoned that he'd hug the land; after all, it's a golden rule, whether you're swimming or in a boat. Or traveling across frozen water. I was thoroughly mistaken, however. He set out across the ice with gusto, using his poles with impressive force and pushing with his skis as hard as he could. I took a few hasty steps. I was drawn toward him, tense, expectant, and horrified all at once. After a couple of minutes, I was down at the edge of the lake. I stood there with my hand shading my eyes, watching that hazardous passage over the ice.

He'd gotten a good way out.

I stared after the long legs in their red tights, and then I noticed something happen. All at once, his steady rhythm changed. He lost speed and seemed to stumble over his skis. At first, I thought he might have hit a rough patch of ice, because he was working his arms very fast; then their movement became frantic. He fell through the ice. As I watched from the shore, he fell through the thin ice on Lake Mester and started sinking. My pulse began to race with a mixture of fear and shock; my whole body felt hot, my cheeks and neck were burning. Now he was struggling in the water like a madman. Suddenly he had the idea of using the spikes on his poles for purchase and dragging himself out like that, but this didn't work because the ice kept breaking. Time and again, flakes, large and small, broke off from the edge. I stood as if turned to stone on the shore and watched the frenzied struggle for life. Simultaneously, I reached for the mobile phone in my pocket, as if there were time enough for that to save him. I certainly wasn't willing to sacrifice my life for some unknown idiot. So I stood there watching in horror, while he fought frantically in the icy water. I heard his screams clearly, and although he was a long way off, their harrowing sound pierced me to my very marrow. His cries wrung me, but I also found them strangely exciting. He should have known better than to cross an ice-covered lake in April, I thought. People generally get what they deserve, don't they? The ice continued to crack beneath his hands. His shouts had lost something of their strength. Sometimes he left off for a few moments. It was clear he was beginning to get chilled because he was moving more slowly in the black water.

You skied as fast as you could over the fields, I mused, as I stood watching.

You were skiing for life.

But death was waiting a little way ahead.

And then, silence.

The dark pool gaped like the jaws of a predator. The man in the red suit had disappeared, swallowed up by the inky water. I stood on the lakeshore panting, my cheeks still flaming hot, for his death throes had also played themselves out in me. I strove to calm my body, my respiration, and my heart. No one else had witnessed what I had seen. For an eternity, I stood there staring. Then I turned and walked quickly homeward, glancing over my shoulder now and again, afraid that he might have risen from the depths again in his red ski-suit. As I walked, I clutched the mobile phone in my pocket. I really should have reported it. But something held me back. An unwillingness to draw attention to myself, to admit that I'd stood there looking on ineffectually, and perhaps be criticized because I hadn't done anything. I hadn't shouted a warning after him as he'd raced over the fields. I could at least have done that. When, forty minutes later, I reached my house at last, I was dizzy and faint. I attempted to digest this new self-awareness, that I was not a man of action. I tried to think clearly, but I was intoxicated by what I'd seen—the man who'd struggled and sunk, screaming with fear and agony. Then, for a while, I imagined his watery death and the pain he'd endured, the feeling of pressure behind his eyes, the fire in his lungs. That it had taken time. The thoughts that had raced through his mind, the dizzying feeling of loneliness in dying out there alone in the cold water. Eventually I collapsed into a chair. I sat there for a long while with my head in my hands. Perhaps he'd noticed me standing on the shore staring. What treachery it must have seemed to him that I hadn't lifted a finger.

It was a long and restless night.

Accusations came from every corner of the room, recriminations from under the bed and threats from up near the ceiling, that I was a miserable and worthless person. That I lacked backbone and any notion of self-sacrifice. At the same time, I was dazzled by it all, as if someone had selected me as sole witness to that awful event. I didn't get to sleep until nearly daybreak, exhausted by everything that had happened. When the light came through the window, I jumped out of bed.

10

I WENT STRAIGHT to the living room and switched on the radio.

When the foreign news was over, they ran a piece about a missing skier, just as I'd expected. The man had gone out for exercise and hadn't come home, they said. They feared he'd gone through the ice. Search parties had found ski tracks on the lake. I listened to all this as I prepared a light breakfast: a couple of slices of whole-grain bread with marmalade, and some really hot, strong coffee, which tasted wonderful. It struck me that I could still call the police and simply mention guardedly that I'd seen a skier dressed in red in the fields close to Lake Mester. But I ate and did nothing; I was excited by the whole event, and a bit troubled at my own reaction. There was a slight rushing in my head, like there used to be when I was a boy and had eaten too much sugar. The sight of the man who went through the ice was mine alone; it was something I wanted to keep to myself. God hadn't seen him, nor yet the devil; only I, Riktor, had that drowning man branded on my memory forever.

Afterward I went to the park.

I sat by the fountain and wrestled with thoughts of life and death. The secret lay there like a shining red mark on my chest, and I imagined that everyone could see it through my clothes. Suddenly a man came walking up the path, big, muscular, and bowed. He took no notice of *Woman Weeping*, but went directly to one of the benches and sat down, slightly hunched, ignoring my modest presence. Right away I felt a little nervous because there was undoubtedly something awe-inspiring about him. His skin and hair were black, and he was dressed in combat gear and tall, black leather boots as if he were fighting a war. I realized immediately that he was from the Refugee Reception Center; it wasn't far away, only ten minutes' walk from the Dixie Café. Where, incidentally, the asylum seekers weren't welcome because they stole things. At least the owner claimed they were a bunch of thieves, stealing candy and other things that were on the counter. People from the Reception Center were often seen wandering along the road. They walked without any object or aim because they had nothing to do—apart from play table tennis, and that soon wears thin. Knocking a ball back and forth over a net isn't much of a challenge. The man suddenly stared in my direction, and I froze and willed myself to become invisible. His eyes were black and hard. There wasn't an iota of friendliness in them, only despondency. I was careful not to return the stare; I didn't want to arouse any violent impulses in him, didn't want to activate that mountain of muscle. Perhaps he was traumatized—that's probably why they come—perhaps he'd seen his own child hacked up with a machete or impaled on a bayonet, you never can tell. And the brutality we hear of in other parts of the world is almost impossible to imagine.

Where's his knife? I wondered, in the midst of my fear, for by now my imagination was running wild. Could it be in his boot, or does he keep it in a pocket? Perhaps it was my turn to face death now, and there were no witnesses. Someone would find me on the ground, bleeding, in front of the bench, with punctured lungs.

Possibly it would be Miranda and her mother, possibly Arnfinn. Maybe I'd be able to crawl down the path to the Dixie Café; sometimes people managed such things even though they were dying. But the black man evinced no interest in me. He just sat wrapped in his own tormented thoughts, his gaze now fixed on his black leather boots. There was something so abject about him—something so wretched and hopeless that in the end I found myself feeling a crumb of sympathy for him, even though sympathy isn't my strong point. Despite that, I was moved. A black giant in combat kit, probably friendless, without home or family, unemployed, and with no rights of any sort. He'd come over here and had been allowed to play table tennis as often as he wanted; that's not much to celebrate. Not that I was especially sympathetic, as I said; they only come over here to help themselves to what we've got.

Suddenly he rose from the bench. I flinched slightly when that great bulk moved so quickly because I was still thinking that he might decide to attack. He might fly at me without provocation. It was always happening; you read about it in the newspapers. The massive body moved away through the trees, walking with a heavy rolling gait, and almost immediately blended in with the leaves. I relaxed once more and followed him with my eyes. To be so big and strong, I thought, and so lonely and miserable. Maybe he was on his way to the Dixie Café to steal candy.

Then Arnfinn came tottering along the path.

He must have encountered the black refugee from the Reception Center, but he showed no sign of it. The alcoholic is indifferent to most things. He lurched over to his usual bench, sat down heavily, and groped automatically in his Windbreaker for his silver hip flask. Remembering it was lost, he patted his other pocket and took out a half-bottle. He put it to his lips and drank. I didn't quite know why, but I approved of the simple life he appeared to lead: sleeping, drinking, pottering around in the park, without cares or responsibilities, other than finding enough to drink. While the rest of us toiled. While the rest of us paid taxes and dragged ourselves from one chore to the next, he sat on his bench drinking a half-bottle of vodka. While the world at large hummed along without him. His eyes were veiled with intoxication, but also with modesty and shame. I don't want to be a burden to anybody, the eyes said, when I nodded affably in his direction. He also had the habit of tilting his head to one side, as if recalling an old memory, and then a smile would soften his ravaged features. He never addressed anyone from his bench. He never apologized and he never asked for the smallest thing. Neither did I for that matter; I minded my own business, as I believe we all should. He took time over his drink, enjoying every last drop. Each time he took a nip, he closed his eyes and the spirit coursed through his veins and warmed him. When the bottle was empty, he got up and left and went home to unconsciousness and oblivion. In all probability, he slept deeply and dreamlessly, and well into the following day. Presumably he missed his hip flask, which was now in my possession. Of course one day, when I was good and ready, I'd return it. But I was in no hurry.

The sight of the man struggling in the water haunted me from hour to hour. Again and again, I saw the ice crack beneath his hands. I saw his arms working like the sails of a windmill; I heard the outraged screams of a man who had been big and strong, but was now in the clutches of death. How much life there is in a human being, I marveled. How much strength, how much will to survive, how much fear for the end of existence and the great darkness. Each time the image projected itself on my inner eye, my pulse increased, but it was also a curse. It reminded me of who I was: someone on the outside of everything, a paltry observer of life. Sometimes, at night, the scene was in close-up, as if I were standing on the edge of the broken ice looking down at him. Then he would stare back at me with burning eyes. As whisperings filled the corners of the room, and that damned truck stood there, its engine turning, filling the bedroom with the acrid smell of diesel fumes.

11

IF ONLY I had a woman!

It gnawed at me, this desire, this longing to be part of a couple. But I'm no good with women. I continued to send Sister Anna long, lingering glances, even though I knew it would never lead to anything. I don't arouse anything in women; bitter experience has taught me that. I've spent my whole life in total solitude. She was off work for a couple of days, but it couldn't have been anything serious because soon she was back again. I was on the late shift and ran across her in the corridor. But she didn't stroke my arm as usual; her eyes were distant, and she passed me without a word. Her indifference was almost unbearable. I was used to a smile and a passing touch, and now I got nothing. I carried on pacing the corridors like a pauper, numbed by my yearning for attention. Life is tough enough as it is, and I need some comfort.

At three o'clock, we had a short meeting. Dr. Fischer sat rubbing his temple as usual. He seemed distant as well, as if his thoughts were somewhere far away from the ward office. He was surprised, he confessed, that some of his many prescriptions weren't having the desired effect. He could hardly have known that I was flushing the tablets down the toilet. And that occasionally, just for fun, I would swap them around, and give Waldemar Rommen the pills that Mr. Larson should have had, and vice versa. It wasn't really of any consequence; but this small, mundane hoax gave me a frisson of excitement because I was making a difference. Here, to explain these destructive tendencies of mine, I could say that my mother used to beat me with a stick. But it wouldn't be true. In reality she was just taciturn and indifferent, only coming out with endless critical saws about how life ought to be lived. We've only ourselves to blame, she would say; you reap what you sow. You've made your bed, now you can lie in it. There was no end to them. But she never hit me. We never had much contact. She was always engrossed in the house and all the things that had to be cleaned and polished, watered, and looked after. I think she felt more for her houseplants than she did for me. There was something about her eyes and her hands when she held a flower between her fingers, a sudden tenderness. I've no idea what made her bring me into the world; presumably it was an accident. These are the tedious thoughts I struggle with as I walk up and down the ward's corridors. With my predilections and my sharp nails.

In and out of the old people's rooms.

Aged wretches, lying in the antechamber of death.

If only there were a bond between me and Anna. A line to Sali Singh, a thin thread between me and Dr. Fischer. Something that kept me right in the world. But I have no such link to others, no ropes holding me to the ground, no hawser to stop me drifting. Once I came across a dog on the road. I was just a small boy then, but the memory is so clear. It stopped to sniff, and I grabbed it firmly by the ears and peered into its yellow eyes, stood there holding it fast. The dog looked back at me with the intensity of a predator. And I discovered something far down in the depths of its black pupils that evoked a sort of resonance deep within me.

That we were distantly related. But it was so fleeting. The dog pulled itself free and vanished, and I was no longer sure of what I'd seen.

Anna is the only one who brings out anything good in me. I follow her around the corridors like a puppy, waiting for her kindly hand, waiting for her scent, her slim feet in their white shoes. But now she seemed distant. Something was distracting her, and I was being excluded.

I often thought that only I inhabited this terrain.

At the foot of this volcano, in the harsh, barren landscape where nothing grows.

12

ONE DAY, WHILE I was sitting alone in the park, surrounded by all the green shoots of spring, Lill Anita came up the path pushing Miranda in her wheelchair. I knew she was called Lill Anita because I'd heard her on her mobile phone. Hi, this is Lill Anita, she'd say, as if her being on the other end of the line was some sort of event in itself. Their approach was silent; the rubber wheels made no noise, but I saw the glint of metal as they came around the bend. They halted at *Woman Weeping*. Lill Anita attempted to explain something using large, clear gestures, and Miranda's uncontrollable hand dabbed at her own hair. They arrived at the bench they always used. The wheelchair was placed where they could reach each other easily, and the brake duly applied. A light pressure on the pedal, and the wheels were locked.

They glanced quickly over at me sitting by myself; they were used to me being on my own. Perhaps they guessed, quite correctly, that I had no one. Not a single person I could call a friend and barely even an acquaintance, apart from my colleagues at Løkka. And I didn't have anything to do with them when I wasn't at work. Mine was a simple existence without any great responsibilities, but there was something missing even so. Sometimes I felt that this need was getting the upper hand. And making me desperate for closeness and companionship. But then it would recede again, and I would take pleasure once more in the freedom and advantages of solitude. I'd never exchanged a single word with Lill Anita; we were only on nodding terms. So I gazed at the fountain and the flowing water. The day held no promise for me; I was just killing time until my next shift.

Miranda was wearing a dress and, because there was a nip in the air, a pair of thick socks as well. They were patterned with some sort of yellow and gray zigzag, reminiscent of a snake. She had a bow in her wispy hair and chalky white sneakers on her feet. Lill Anita was clad in studded jeans. The faded denim had several large tears in the thighs, so you could see the pale skin beneath. With all those studs, and a good deal of piercing too, she resembled a bed of nails. This apart, she was nice enough, with a wan, heart-shaped face and a pouting, pink mouth that I assumed would be quick to purse in sarcasm if she were annoyed. She tapped eagerly away on her mobile phone, busy sending a text message. Her fingers, slender as noodles and tipped with black nail polish, worked rapidly. Miranda was left to her own devices. Her eyes rolled up in her head, and she slipped slightly over to one side; there wasn't much backbone in that frail body. Occasionally she would bend backward in a spasm. I wondered where they came from, these involuntary movements. Now Lill Anita began a telephone conversation, and I listened keenly. I could hardly do otherwise, as her words wafted in my direction. Her voice cut through the air. It had a particular, sharp edge.

"Hi, it's Lill Anita here. Yes, we're in the park. Oh, God no, it's not easy finding something to do every damn day. And I don't like going to the Dixie. People stare and I'm so sick of it. Miranda's just the same as other kids. She always starts making a fuss, then people gawk even more; I can't bear it. Yes. We've just arrived. Well, the weather's not too bad. Might as well sit here as anywhere. What did you say? You're at the Dixie? Have you got that film we were talking about? Is it on Blu-ray? Is it as good as every-one says? Can I borrow it?"

Here Lill Anita paused. She tended the child with a busy hand, smoothing her hair and straightening her dress. She checked if she was cold; I don't think she was. Then she looked over at me sitting on my bench. It was as if a thought had suddenly struck her, as if she'd seen me for the very first time. Her gaze was long, sober, and appraising. It took in the whole of me: my slicked-back hair and my thin, stooping shoulders.

"Sorry to trouble you," she said in a high, carrying voice, be-cause I was some way off, and the water from the fountain made a certain amount of noise. "Sorry to trouble you, but I've got to nip over to the Dixie quickly to fetch something. You couldn't keep an eye on Miranda for me while I'm away, could you?"

She leaned over the wheelchair and straightened Miranda's dress again. It was a beautiful dress; I don't know how people can dress their children up like that when they're on Social Security. She was doubtless on Social Security too, just like the alcoholic Arnfinn. That's what the system's come to now; you can manage for a long time without a job. Some people spend a whole lifetime without contributing to society.

"It'll only take ten minutes," she added. "I'll run all the way."

She gazed at me under mascaraed lashes and gave the small pout of a wheedling child. As for me, I was completely dumbstruck. I couldn't believe my ears. Miranda, that helpless, speechless child, in my depraved custody. The two of us alone in the park by Lake Mester—a little disabled girl entrusted to me and my whims, and my defective impulse control. I checked the surrounding park several times. No one else was in sight, just a few sparrows hop-ping around searching for food at the base of the fountain. They found nothing, only candy wrappings and other bits of litter. De-composing leaves from the previous year were rustling along the ground, and there was a soughing from the trees lining the paved path. A gust of wind blew through the park, ruffling my hair; quickly, I patted it down.

Keep an eye on Miranda. Had I heard her correctly? I took myself sternly in hand, making an effort to appear responsible. How long had we both been coming to the park by Lake Mester, Lill Anita and I? For at least a year, regularly. I had always behaved in a respectable manner. I was well dressed, too, in a decent jacket and trousers. And, as I've said, we were on nodding terms.

"I'll look after Miranda," I promised, and rose from my bench. I walked calmly across the parterre, with slow, measured steps and open, candid hands. Although my head was seething. Although my fingers were itching and my whole body was tingling, I kept calm. That feeble, gesticulating child. In my care. Lill Anita jumped up right away. She finished her conversation and slipped the mobile phone in her pocket. She nodded at the path and over toward the café.

"Ten minutes tops," she repeated. "I'm only going to collect a film. You don't have to speak; she's so hard to understand, I mean, for anyone except me. Just sit quietly on the bench. If she tries to wheel herself away, you'll have to stop her. She can be a bit difficult sometimes, but the brake is on. Make sure of the brake," she said breathlessly.

Then she ran off down the paved path. She ran past *Woman Weeping* in her studded, faded jeans, and then she was gone.

The wheelchair was a Plesner and seemed well equipped.

At the back, there was a colorful netting pouch that contained some clothes, a knitted jacket, and a threadbare teddy with eyes of black glass. It was old and covered in burls, and quite smelly when I put it to my nose. But the child smelled of soap. It had a scent that was sweet, like wildflowers. Her sneakers were clean and white; she couldn't walk in them, so their only function was to keep her feet warm. The laces were tied with a double bow. She immediately became restive when I seated myself on the bench—restive because her mother wasn't there, and because she didn't know me. I could read it in the attitude of her thin neck, and from the hands that fluttered over her lap. I didn't speak a word; I waited. The silence made her uneasy. One can relate to words, but thoughts can't be monitored. She was probably used to the various clumsy comments people make: what a lovely wheelchair you've got, can I see your teddy bear? Or similar inanities. Five minutes passed. I sat absolutely still on the bench with my hands in my lap, while my imagination ran wild. Miranda's head lolled back and she opened her mouth. I could see her large front teeth, big as sugar lumps. Her feet in their white sneakers were turned inward, and a wide belt held her in the wheelchair. It was fastened with a shiny buckle.

I glanced at the path. Lill Anita wasn't in sight. So I quickly dived into my pocket where I had a packet of lozenges. I opened the packet and took one out, weighing it in my hand. It was a Fisherman's Friend. Small, sand-colored, and oval, and so strong it brought tears to the eyes. And, seeing as Miranda was sitting there gaping like a baby thrush, I popped it into her mouth. At first nothing happened. The lozenge lay on her tongue where it slowly but surely began to melt, and to wreak its overpowering havoc. Then the first tears appeared. Some saliva ran down her chin and onto the front of her dress, while I kept an eye out for Lill Anita who would shortly appear on the paved path. Miranda struggled desperately with the strong lozenge. She attempted to expel it with her tongue, but this proved too much for her limited powers of coordination; she couldn't manage it. There's something about drooling. It makes people appear moronic, but for all I knew this gasping little girl might be as sharp as the scythe I had at home. A sudden light in her eyes told me that her mother was coming at last. I rose from the bench and smiled soothingly. Assured her that everything was fine. Lill Anita ran the final few steps across the parterre.

"Have you given her something to eat?"

She rummaged in the net at the back of the chair for some tissue, tore off a large piece, and wiped Miranda's mouth.

"Only a piece of candy," I said in my defense.

Her cheeks turned bright red. Presumably caused by a mixture of annoyance and shame, because she'd left her helpless child in the care of an unknown man who looked like a pike.

"You mustn't give her anything," she said angrily, "or it could stick in her throat. Good God! You mustn't give her things; are you crazy or what?"

So that's the thanks you get, I thought, and stared at the object she'd deposited on the bench. A DVD.

Presumably she was going to watch it when evening finally arrived and Miranda was asleep. Those few, precious nighttime hours without responsibility. I returned to my own bench, and they began making rapid preparations to leave. Lill Anita put the film in the net, released the brake, spun the wheelchair around, and set off down the paved path.

Serves you right for leaving your child with a stranger, I said to myself. You wicked, slovenly woman.

13

ONE NIGHT SOON after, I dreamed about the man in the red ski-suit.

I was standing on the lakeshore and saw him fall through. I tried to shout, but I was mute and no sound came from me. It was terrible to watch his furious battle in the water, his constant thrashing and clawing attempts to pull himself out. Yet I also felt a strange thrill, as if I were full of good adrenaline, pumping my blood at tremendous speed through my veins. They've searched the lake for him without success. The rescue services and some volunteers. It must be hard for his relatives, I thought, knowing that he's lying at the bottom of the lake, decomposing. His skin becoming porous, the flesh loosening from his bones, fish eating their way in through his eye sockets.

Ever since the episode with Miranda and the Fisherman's Friend, Lill Anita has been somewhat reserved. But she still comes to the park. She occupies the bench as if it belongs to her. She's on her mobile phone for much of the time, always keeping an eye on the girl in the wheelchair. For Miranda is there the whole time, every moment needy and dependent. Ebba has been over a few times and patted her on the cheek. As if that were of any use. But old ladies are like that; they always make a fuss about petty things.

· · ·

Often, when I'm at work and have a bit of time to spare, I go out to the kitchen and see Sali Singh. With his brightly colored clothes and his expansive, barrel-shaped body, he reminds me of a Russian matryoshka doll. In which case, there would be six smaller Salis inside the outer one; it's a fascinating thought. And there do seem to be several of him too, a different one each day. He's inscrutable. We talk about the state of the world, and all the things, good and bad, that affect us human beings. Sali is a gentle soul, full of Indian wisdom, and I enjoy listening to his calm, deep voice with its quaint accent. He often gives me a bit of food, perhaps a taster from the day's menu or a small cake. He puts it in a bowl and pushes it across the table to me. He's kind and generous and has no ulterior motives.

Then there's Sister Anna, beautiful little Anna.

One day she came walking wearily into the ward office. She slumped into a chair and propped her head on her hand. The sun was pouring through the window and made her hair glow. I could see she was suffering. That she was ruminating on something serious, and that it was making her strangely distant. But then the mood passed and she pulled herself together; she's nothing if not an indomitable woman. She reminded us that old Waldemar Rommen was celebrating his birthday that day. He was ninety-eight, believe it or not. It was practically a provocation in itself; there was almost no life left in him. His heart gave a beat occasionally, and now and then a shallow breath would pass his lips. His hands and feet were ice cold and had blue, bunched veins; his cheeks were as pale as marble. But Anna spent the day treating him in every conceivable way. For her, birthdays are sacrosanct; let no one deny it. But ninety-eight. Hardly any respiration or circulation, hardly any intake of food or drink, almost mummified, dry and tough as driftwood. Despite all this, Anna sat in a chair at his bedside and chatted for a long time. A quiet prattle that elicited no answer. She lit candles and brought in the flowers his family had sent by courier, asters. I've never liked them; they're vulgar. Waldemar Rommen has dementia. He understood nothing of what was going on, but Anna wanted to make much of him anyway. I visited Waldemar as well several times that day. He turned away when he saw me coming and seemed inexpressibly tired, the shriveled face impassive.

I sat in a chair by the bed, grasped his bony hand, and held it firmly.

"This is your last birthday," I said. "Take my word for it."

If he felt pain or sorrow about what I'd said, he hadn't the strength to formulate it. But his eyes were full of water. I pulled my hand away and went out again, and carried on with my duties. We have so many patients on our ward, and there's a long waiting list as well. Lots of people who want our costly care and our services.

I kept my eye on Anna all that day.

She went around wrapped in her own thoughts and was obviously working through something difficult, because her eyes were somber and her mouth had a sorrowful slant. I didn't want to meddle and pry—I know how to behave—but I wanted to get her alone in the ward office. It took some time before an opportunity presented itself at last. Naturally, Dr. Fischer came in and sat on and on, with his legs crossed, joggling his foot. He had the obligatory suede shoes on and, as usual, he massaged his temple. We could never hear him coming. He'd steal along the corridors like an Indian hunter.

At last we sat there, Anna and I, on each end of the sofa. It was just the two of us; Dr. Fischer had left. She closed her eyes and nodded off. I saw her chest rise and fall in a slow, heavy rhythm.

The sun flooded in through the window and her lovely face was bathed in an almost ethereal light. Suddenly she opened her eyes.

"I'm not quite myself," she mumbled. "Do excuse me."

Then she shut her eyes again and rested her head against the wall. And I realized that something had happened. My imagination set to work. It's probably her husband, I thought. He wants a divorce; he's found another woman. I studied her hand clandestinely, but saw that her wedding ring was still there. You never can tell, though; the relationship between two people is a difficult thing. "What are you then, if you're not yourself?" I asked tentatively.

"I'm upset," she said quietly. "It's my brother, Oscar."

"What's wrong with Oscar?" I asked. "Is he ill?"

"He fell through the ice on Lake Mester," she replied. "And they can't find him."

14

MY BROTHER OSCAR fell through the ice.

I hadn't misheard; she really had said it.

Then she got up and went out. She drifted down the corridor, her skirt swinging gently around her slim legs. Her brother, I thought. Her brother Oscar in the red ski-suit—he who'd battled against the water and lost, and I'd witnessed it. There was a bond between us after all. I saw it clearly. Destiny had a plan; this couldn't be coincidence. There was something larger than me, a pattern that I was part of, and its discovery thrilled me and made me dizzy all at once.

I carried my secret with me for the rest of the day. Now it was even bigger, and I felt ready to burst like an overinflated balloon. But the truth had to be withheld; I had to bear that alone. However, I felt I'd been chosen. I was the only one who knew.

When the shift was over and evening was approaching, I went to the park. That day I took a detour and arrived at the fountain from a different direction, along a path that skirted the lake and then led on to the town, with all its bustle. This took me past the other beautiful sculpture in the park by Lake Mester.

Woman Laughing. I stood for a while regarding her. I put my hand on the smooth bronze and ran it over her thighs and back in

45

long affectionate strokes. Having first checked over my shoulder to make sure no one was looking at me. Then I went to my bench and sat down, admiring the dolphins and listening to the chuckling water. I sat there alone with my big secret, this new discovery in my life: I was one of the chosen.

I sat there until evening began to descend.

The darkness crept slowly on, but with my exceptional night vision, I saw the shapes and outlines start to quiver with their familiar light. A sparrow, a stray cat, insects—like fireflies, all of them. And then came the calm that dusk brings with it, of everything settling down, of everything ceasing. My own breathing was all that could be heard. I was just about to get up and go. Home to the empty house and its empty rooms, home to the diesel engine that was impossible to escape, home to the whispering voices.

Just then, Arnfinn came tottering along the path.

Slow, heavy, and swaying, he struggled to keep on his feet. But it was obvious that he was bound for his bench, the one he usually occupied. I sat there serenely and watched his labored progress. Either he'd drunk too much, or too little. He came on, rocking like an injured crow, limping, uncertain and helpless, impervious to the fact that I was sitting there studying him. His hands groped for support, but his main problem was his trembling; the whole of the faltering edifice was threatening to collapse at any moment. But he walked. One foot in front of the other, his bloodshot eyes fixed on the green bench. At last he lowered himself onto it. For a while, he sat there blinking, not even looking in my direction. Then all at once he brightened, as if he'd thought of something pleasant. He rummaged in his inside pocket for the hip flask, which always used to accompany him, which always used to provide peace and warmth. The lovely, silver-plated hip flask, which was now in my inside pocket—the trophy I'd taken and carried with me ever since. Waiting for the right moment. And the moment was now.

This was the decisive instant when I would finally come to his rescue. I would come like a savior and light up those bloodshot eyes; I would help his trembling body to relax. I'd never been a softhearted soul, but here was a man I could save. Anna's brother drowned before my eyes, but now I could make a difference. I rose and went over to him, took the hip flask from my pocket, and offered it with a smile and a friendly nod. The feeling of doing a good deed spread upward from my toes and suffused my whole body. He took it and studied it carefully, to see if it really was the hip flask he'd missed so sorely. He managed to remove the top after a bit of a struggle, but there was only a drop left in the flask, not sufficient to satisfy his need. Nevertheless, he went on putting the flask to his lips, as if hoping for some miracle that might fill it with vodka, providing he didn't stop hoping.

"You haven't got a drink, by any chance?" he asked feebly.

The asking had cost him dearly. He was now staring at the ground, but his need was too great; he had to bite the bullet and beg.

"Yes," I said, "I've got a drink. I've got a bottle of vodka. And, you know, it could be for you."

I took hold of his arm and hauled him up. He was as unmanageable as a sack of potatoes. At that moment, I caught his smell, a mixture of mildew and drunkenness. He hung heavily on my arm, and I was scared he'd fall on the path and lie there floundering. But he managed. Walking like a wounded soldier, heading for vodka and salvation. I was used to doing this, of course, walking and supporting someone on my arm, like the few patients at Løkka who were able to get around.

"A drink," I reiterated. "To put you back together again."

He replied with a few snuffling noises. Keeping on the move was occupying all his efforts, but he was driven on by the thought of relief. As we walked, I tried to come to terms with what I was doing, and what my plan was, why I'd followed this sudden impulse to take him home with me. And treat him to my vodka. It must have had something to do with an intractable loneliness. I tried to recall the last time someone had sat on my sofa. I couldn't think of anyone, apart from a vacuum-cleaner salesman long ago, and he was only interested in demonstrating his fantastic machine. Which, by the way, I didn't buy because it was far too expensive. Apart from him, a few Poles had come to the door with drawings that they tried to sell to help pay for their education here in Norway. But I never bought any of the drawings, either. To be honest, I was never very impressed with them; I thought I could have done better myself, had I taken the trouble to sit down with a pencil and paper. There'd just never been the opportunity, but I suspected I might have a hidden talent in that department. I hauled and steered and supported Arnfinn along the paved path past *Woman Weeping* and the Dixie Café. We met no one on our shuffling progress, nor did we speak. We walked, ponderous and unsteady, a sorry sight in the gloaming, and it was as if both of us understood our goal: a drink and a bit of pleasant company.

Several times he almost fell.

Once, he lurched out into the road, and then almost slipped into the ditch, while I gripped his arm and tried to steer him in the right direction. The journey from the park to Jordahl, which usually takes half an hour, took us forty-five minutes. When at last he realized we'd arrived, he seemed unspeakably relieved. He clumped up the steps, all five of them, leaning heavily on the handrail. He stood clinging to it as I unlocked the door, and then staggered through the hall into my small, spartan living room. It felt odd bringing someone home with me. A stranger within my private domain, breathing my air, gazing at my things, my furniture, and experiencing my taste for meticulous order. For no one came to my house, and that was entirely my own fault. Now the habit was about to be broken; I had a guest. An alcoholic from the park by Lake Mester, but he was better than nothing.

"You mentioned something about a drink," said Arnfinn.

He coughed, putting a hand up to his mouth. He had taken a seat on the sofa and pressed himself into the corner, his large hands lying motionless in his lap.

"Yes," I said. "You'll get your drink. But I'm not having any. I think it's a dreadful habit and I don't drink."

He laughed a little uncertainly at this. He tried to curb his violent trembling and peered around him as if searching for the bottle I'd been tempting him with. Perhaps they're communing, I thought, on some special frequency. Perhaps the bottle is transmitting an almost imperceptible signal from the cupboard, and it's striking Arnfinn's aura.

"We could play 'You're getting hot,'" I suggested, and smiled agreeably.

All of a sudden, he looked shamefaced and stared down at his hands. His nails had dark edges, and there wasn't much doubt that those hands had done their fair share of hard work.

"Not playing," he mumbled reluctantly.

He sat there with his Windbreaker on, refusing to take it off.

"No," I said. "I was just joking. You're not a child. You're unemployed, aren't you? Are you on Social Security? I'm not trying to be rude; I'm simply interested. Are you on the dole, Arnfinn? You needn't be afraid of divulging things to me. I'm a member of one of the caring professions. I'm used to all that. I mean, people needing help."

He shrugged his shoulders and turned away slightly, trying to get comfortable in the corner of the sofa. His gaze had begun to

49

wander, as if he regretted coming and wanted to go again. Perhaps now he couldn't quite grasp how he'd ended up in my living room. He felt his pocket again but remembered that the hip flask was empty.

"Is there something you want?" he asked.

I sat looking at him for a long time before I replied.

"Company," I said simply. "Not many people come to this house. But I've always got a bottle in the cupboard," I added, "just in case. A case like yours. And it's nice to have something to offer. Of course you'll get a drink. I'm feeling generous. I don't often feel that way, but you've caught me on a good day."

He managed a brave smile. His cheeks flushed with pleasure. Then I rose and went to the cupboard, fetched the bottle and glass. He heard the chink, and immediately it brought him to life; light shone at last in his somber gaze. I held the bottle out to him and pointed to the label.

"Perhaps this isn't the sort you're used to?"

I set it on the table in front of him.

He nodded eagerly and assured me that the brand was absolutely excellent; then he leaned forward. His hands began creeping in the direction of the bottle, like a brace of starving animals. But he pulled himself together and straightened his back as if, from somewhere deep in his mind, where his reason lay, he realized I was playing a game, and that he would have to play along whether he wanted to or not. If he wanted his reward, the assuaging liquor. He smiled, showing yellow, somewhat worn teeth, clasped his hands in his lap, and waited. So, I poured out some vodka for him, and he drank. He held the glass in both hands like a small child. The effect was like pouring oil into a machine that has ground to a halt. Immediately his head came up, and his eyes sparkled with new luster. His hand became steady; it was a miracle.

I let him sit in peace for a while and drink. I watched him as he raised the glass and put it to his lips.

"What's the situation?" I asked, when I saw that he'd achieved a bit of equilibrium and the warmth of the spirit had spread through his body. "Is there someone waiting for you at home? Have you got a family?"

He made no reply to this but drank more vodka. He was only focused on the glass. He'd already forgotten that I was sitting there, or so it seemed; only the intoxication was important now. At all costs he had to arrive at a state of oblivion, and he wasn't the slightest bit concerned that there would be a witness to his shame.

"I've never married," I explained. "I can't seem to manage it. Everyone else can, but I only end up knocking around here on my own. I've been on my own for years; it's extraordinary, isn't it? I mean, how can it be that difficult?"

He remembered I was there. He sat studying me with glistening eyes. All the while clasping his glass in both hands, like a predator guarding its prey.

"You can't go to expensive shops if you haven't got money," he declared.

After dropping this philosophical remark, he applied himself to the vodka again. I sat pondering for a while and then came to the conclusion that he'd just insulted me, but I decided to keep calm. For Anna was undoubtedly worth a good deal, and I wasn't exactly handsome, so he had a point. A swan and a pike can never pair up.

"All I do is look most of the time," I admitted. "And then I dream a bit. Dreaming is free." I inclined my head. "And what about you, Arnfinn?" I said. "Do you dream as well? About this or that?"

He raised his face in surprise. He was still clutching his glass. They were as one now, he and the bottle. He was on a tryst with

51

his best friend, alcohol. And it was clearly an everlasting love affair, or so it seemed to me.

"There must be something you want," I said. "Everyone wants something. I mean, all our lives are missing one thing or another, and you're no exception surely?"

He shook his head emphatically.

"I don't want anything," he said. "I just drift along. I'm not bothered about anything; what will be, will be. *You* can want something, if you like. You're not a slave to alcohol, so presumably you haven't lost your head."

I agreed. Naturally I hadn't lost my head. I unscrewed the cap of the bottle and filled his glass to the brim.

"Have you got an excuse?" I inquired. "An excuse for drinking, I mean?"

The question made him look up.

"Excuse? Do I need one?"

"I'm only curious," I explained. "People often have a kind of explanation for why things have turned out the way they have. Why they're violent, why they drink, why they steal. That sort of stuff."

Arnfinn took another drink. It gurgled in his gullet. Suddenly he seemed utterly content, both with himself and his own existence. He was out visiting and he was getting a drink. Things couldn't get any better; this was life at its best.

"Life's pretty good," he said. "My check comes every month. I drop in to the liquor store, and then squat on a park bench. Go back home and sleep. And that's about it."

"You've certainly got a routine," I said, "but it's a bit of a lazy life. Drinking all day, then crashing out in the evening. While the rest of us work."

At this, his features took on a bitter cast.

"What should I worry about the rest of the world for? I didn't ask to be born."

All at once the mere idea of life seemed to do him an injustice, as if I'd reminded him of something unpleasant, something he wanted to forget. That life was a sentence, that he was serving it day by day as he crept toward death, and that his days were without light or warmth. I filled his glass for the third time. He was beginning to relax properly now; he leaned back on the sofa and, for the first time, took in his surroundings.

"This place has never known a woman's touch," he pronounced.

"You're sharp too," I replied. "No, women don't ever come to visit me here. I'm a lone wolf. Just like you."

His gaze, shining now, swept over the room and took everything in. All the telling details that bore witness to who I was.

"Why have you got an Advent star in your window?" he asked, pointing. "It's almost the middle of May."

"But I've pulled the plug out," I said in my own defense. "I pull it out on the first of January and plug it in again on the first of December and, hey presto, it's Christmas. I like doing things the easy way. Just like you. Help yourself to another drink," I coaxed, and nodded toward the bottle. "The drink's all right, isn't it? And you might as well fill your hip flask while you're at it, so you'll have something to keep you going when you wake up tomorrow."

Arnfinn nodded and drank deeply. I thought I was an excellent host, despite my lack of experience. I poured the vodka and let him talk about himself and his life.

"Why don't you switch the light on?" he asked, after a long silence. "It's so dark."

I didn't mention my excellent night vision. I switched on a light above the sofa. The hours went quickly by, as having a visitor was a totally novel experience. A stranger, admittedly, but we would gradually get to know each other, if he should decide to return; I was fairly certain he would. Then he told me about all the black days, about his bad back, which was bad enough for him to claim long-term disability; about all the countries he'd been to, all the ports, as he put it; all the women who'd come and gone, and all of them *had* gone because, as Arnfinn pensively assured me, taking a pull at his glass, nothing good lasts. He drank himself into great glittering halls of light and laughter and warmth. When, after four hours, he finally left and the vodka bottle was empty, I stood at the front door watching him go. He vacillated on the driveway for a moment, shining like a torch, unsure, almost, if he really did want to go. Perhaps I had another bottle, and maybe his journey home was a long one. I stood at the top of the steps and was aware of something new.

Arnfinn, I could say when I went to work. Oh yes, he's an old friend of mine; he often pops in for a visit. I felt happy, standing there on the steps. I liked this new condition of having a friend. He was an alcoholic, it was true, but that was better than nothing.

"Will you be all right getting home?" I inquired.

He coughed contemptuously and began walking.

"You're talking to an old skipper," he said.

Then he continued down the road and vanished.

A lone, burning soul.

15

IT WAS TOO light and too hot in summer. The days never ended and I couldn't stand all the germinating and sprouting and growing. It was like an unbridled force, a cornucopia without meaning: worms that peered out during wet weather, flies and wasps, ladybirds and lice, moths and daddy-long-legs in the curtains, spiders in the corners, mice in the wall. I could hear them scratching. They swarmed, crept, or crawled, and because my thoughts got badly disrupted, I slowly went mad.

I gradually realized that something was taking shape deep within me. An incomprehensible longing whose contours I was in the process of discerning. I wanted to be something. Become something, mean something, be on everyone's lips like a bitter pill. It wasn't enough to wander up and down Løkka's corridors pinching Nelly Friis or whispering nasty threats in Waldemar Rommen's ear. It wasn't enough. I was a nobody. I was totally insignificant—nothing to look at, nothing to the world at large, eminently forgettable—and this knowledge was insufferable. I wanted people to turn and watch me pass, remember me and speak of me with reverence and respect. This yearning grew big. It filled my heart and head. Cost what it might, I had to make a difference. In some way or other, I had to check nature's headlong rush.

Like cutting branches off a tree.

Like pouring poison down a well.

It was as if I'd fallen in a river. I was going with the current as fragments of images flitted past my mind's eye. Like pennants in a summer breeze. Images of Arnfinn with his glass raised. Images of Oscar falling through the ice, images of Ebba with her crocheting, images of Miranda with her thin ankles. Images of Sister Anna, my angel, my little sugarplum.

If only I had a woman!

I went around observing life and its people. I pulled Nelly's hair and pinched her behind the ears, and all the while I listened for signals. Alertness was vital. I liked strolling past the slumbering houses close to where I lived. I liked going to the park by Lake Mester, preferably in the dark when no one could see me. But I could see. Eyes gleaming in the shrubbery behind the benches: foxes, cats, and hares, quivering, darting, orange-colored creatures. I also registered that the big black man from the Reception Center frequently occupied a bench at night. He probably got out of a window, and then sat there on the bench glowing like a house on fire. I stood motionless in the bushes and stared at all that strength that no one wanted.

There was something genuinely pathetic about him. I was not a compassionate person, but that massive man touched something deep within me. He was so very big and so very unwanted.

It came to pass just as I'd imagined.

One day there was an impatient ring at the door.

The sound of the bell through the house was so rare that I jumped, but I'd been waiting. I was no fool; some things were so obvious. I'd dangled a worm and now the fish had bitten. The bell was a harbinger of something new and different, something resembling an occasion in my uneventful life: I was wanted for something. Arnfinn stood at the top of the steps, faltering and shaky as always. With one hand on the wall to steady himself, he looked at me with beseeching eyes. He'd had to swallow his pride, because his need was too great. His dignity had been laid aside; he needed first aid.

"You wouldn't happen to have a drink, would you?" he asked expectantly.

His hopeful inquiry hung in the air between us. I didn't answer immediately; I liked the situation and I wanted to milk it a bit. So I stood for a while in silence and regarded the pathetic figure, the broken-down man in his Windbreaker and stout brown shoes. With his florid face and all his forlorn despair. There was definitely a mutual understanding between us; I felt it clearly as I stood in the open doorway. Deep in his ravaged, drink-sodden brain, Arnfinn had registered that I wanted him for some reason, that he had something I needed. Or, to be more precise, that I had a plan. Even if he didn't understand my motive, the reward was a few glasses of vodka, and vodka was the only thing that got him from one day to the next. I opened the door wide and led the way into the house. He scuttled in after me with his rolling gait and found his place on the sofa, right up in the corner. He sat there, hunched and clasping his hands in his lap, like some inscrutable riddle. He didn't remove his Windbreaker or his shoes, but seated himself as he was. Shabby, unkempt, and thirsty. His eyes turned to the cupboard and, just like the last time, it contained a bottle. I'd bought another in case he dropped in, and he'd realized this. But I didn't hasten across the floor to fetch it. I wanted to wait a bit; I wanted to torment him, at least for a short while. I was like a small boy with a stick, and he was wriggling like a worm.

"Yes, you're thirsty, I expect," I remarked mildly.

Because I could be extremely friendly when I wanted to be, and

I wanted to be then. I dug into my reserves of goodwill, buried deep within me, and which on rare occasions I required.

He dropped his gaze immediately. And coughed to clear his throat.

"I was in the area," he said. "It was too good an opportunity not to visit. For a chat, I mean. If that's not too much to ask. But perhaps your cupboard's empty anyway? I don't want to beg," he maintained. "Well, it was only a thought. I don't want to be a nuisance. But you know how it is; you understand people. I knew that the first moment I set eyes on you."

He was silent for a long time after expressing this piece of flattery. He was sitting right on the edge of the sofa, twining his fingers. Just as scruffy and disheveled as always, with his heavy, stooped body. For an instant, I felt contempt that he couldn't lift himself out of his state and make something of himself, contribute something to society. But then, deep down, I had a liking for him, with his quiet, modest demeanor. There was something honest and decent about his simple existence that I valued. And, after all, I'd already begun tapping those reserves of goodwill. For a while, we sat there in silence. I could see that he was struggling with his thoughts, that he was trying to put them into words, that he actually had something he wanted to say. His eyes wandered over to the Advent star in the window, and it brought a wan smile to his solemn face.

Then his eyes settled on the cupboard once more, in the hope that I might have a bottle. I saw the yearning like a light in those dark eyes. But he bit it back, clinging to the last shred of his dignity: He wanted me to do the offering. I would too. Soon, once he'd sat there and stewed for a bit.

"I want to tell you something," he began, fixing me with his gaze. "Just so you know how things really stand. I'll tell you about something that happened a very long time ago. To a small boy who I know a bit about. That is, if you want to hear it."

"I want to hear," I said. "Fire away."

I sat still and listened attentively, noticing all the while how his eyes constantly darted toward the cupboard.

"He was about six years old," Arnfinn began. "Well, five or six, knee-high, you know, with skinny legs. He was in bed asleep one summer night, with the window open. He slept alone. He had no brothers or sisters, so it was just him. Before he went to sleep, he heard the trees outside. There was a bit of a breeze, you know what I mean, rustling in the treetops, the way that tends to make us sleepy. He was lying with his back to the window and he couldn't hear anything except the trees. At last his eyes closed. Well, don't ask me if he dreamed, because I don't know. All I know is that the big house was completely quiet. And that his mother was sleeping in the room next door."

Arnfinn paused. He thought for a moment and scratched his chin.

"In the middle of the night, he awoke with a terrified scream."

"Why?" I asked. "What had happened?"

"He screamed," Arnfinn repeated. "It reverberated through the house. And his mother was up in an instant, running to his room. Switched on the light. Stood staring at him as he lay beneath the duvet. And you know, he was as white as the sheets he lay in. 'What's the matter?' his mother asked. 'Why did you scream? My God, you made me jump!'

"The boy pointed to the foot of the bed. 'There's a snake under the duvet,' he said. Or rather, I should say he whispered it, because she could only just hear what he said. But she almost collapsed with relief. She was expecting something different, you see. This was something she understood. And then she assumed the look the boy knew so well, the sympathetic look, you know. And it was quite a resigned look too, because he had a lively imagination. Perhaps she thought, kids are kids, and they do say funny things. 'You're having a nightmare,' she said. 'Now, wake up!' She patted him consolingly on the cheek. Then she pulled the duvet off him."

Arnfinn wrung his hands so hard in his lap that his finger joints cracked.

"She pulled the duvet off," he said. "And there between the boy's thin legs lay a huge snake."

Then he stopped again and nodded.

"A huge snake," he repeated.

"You're joking," I interjected.

"I never joke," said Arnfinn. "What would I do that for? It was a snake and it was enormous. Not one of those little ones. It was enormous. It had twisted itself into a great coil. It was black, with a sort of yellowish-gray, speckled pattern, thick as a grown man's arm, and as long as a wet week. His mother could make out its head between the boy's knees—its nasty, flat head. Have you seen a snake close up? They're as ugly as sin, I'm sure you'll agree. The last thing in the world she wanted to do was touch that snake, but she damn well had to, because the boy was completely hysterical. So she grabbed hold of the huge thing and yanked. And you know," said Arnfinn, "when we're frightened, we're tremendously strong. The snake crashed to the floor with a horrible sound and quickly slid under the bed and coiled up. Then she grabbed the boy and fled from the room. Called the police and sat waiting with the boy on her lap. When they came they weren't too keen either, once they saw the horrible creature under the bed. But they had to do something. They put on protective gloves and hauled the snake out, shoving the monstrous thing into a sack. Then they drove off with the snake in the back of the car. Well, what do you think?"

Arnfinn sank back on the sofa. He'd obviously finished his story and seemed tired.

"Very good," I said calmly. "Is there a point to it?"

"There certainly is a point," said Arnfinn. "That snake had escaped from one of the neighboring houses, where a man had been keeping it as a pet. Then it got in through the open window and was attracted to the warmth under the duvet on the boy's bed. Ever since that night, he's found it extremely hard to sleep. He's nearly sixty now, and he's still got problems sleeping."

Here Arnfinn paused for a while. He was waiting for me to say something; it was probably my turn.

"So was it you?" I asked, and now my interest was genuine, because the story about the snake was both compelling and a bit exotic.

"You asked me why I drink," he said. "It doesn't take much. That's all I'm trying to say."

"Did you find a snake in your bed?" I asked. "When you were a boy. Is it a true story?"

"I have problems sleeping," he repeated mulishly.

He gesticulated with open hands. He'd clearly given me what he had to give, and now at last I went to the cupboard and fetched the bottle of vodka. I poured a stiff one and pushed it toward him.

"It's none of my business why you drink," I said generously. "And it's none of your business why I do the things I do. But people always want to go around rubbing shoulders with each other. Confiding, understanding, explaining. Let's skip all that, shall we? We're grown-ups after all."

Arnfinn raised the glass of vodka to his mouth, and now he looked blissful.

"But you've probably got a tale to tell too," he suggested. "About a small boy."

I shook my head emphatically. At the same time, I saw how Arnfinn's face softened and turned gentle and friendly.

"I've never been a small boy," I explained.

Arnfinn chuckled good-naturedly. His body had become loose and relaxed, and he rocked as he sat on the sofa. He was migrating into those bright, shining halls again.

"Never been a small boy," he mimicked. "Now I've heard everything."

"I haven't a single childhood memory," I explained.

He was a little taken aback by my obstinacy.

"Were you ill or something?" he asked.

"As I said," I reiterated, "I can't remember very much at all. Apart from a little shit at school who called me a pike. Well, and I do remember my confirmation. And everything in between is missing. It's simply missing."

Arnfinn's eyes opened wide in amazement.

"But I do have a memory," I added. "Of my mother. A skirt with two legs. And a pair of big shoes. Everything farther up passed me by. Hands. Heart. Head. I mean, they were there all right, but I never managed to get hold of them. D'you know what she used to say? You're always strongest when you're on your own. That was the way I was raised."

"Yes, it's just one damn unending struggle," Arnfinn opined, but his tone was jocular now; the vodka had made him happy and turned his cheeks red. "My bodywork's in terrible condition," he went on, "ugly, dented, and rusty. But my heart ticks over like an old Opel engine. I bet that when my chassis has fallen to pieces, that motor will still be humming along. I get my strong heart from my mother. My God, how it beats."

He placed a hand on his chest and cocked his head.

"And what do you get from your father?" I asked.

Arnfinn pondered the question for a long time.

"This here," he said, raising his glass. "He drank himself to death. Mind if I refill my hip flask?"

16

NATURALLY I REFILLED his hip flask.

Naturally I stroked and humored him as if he were a lost dog. I listened to all his stories: both those that showed him in a good light, and those that showed him in a less flattering one, as a parasite. The narrative about the curse of alcohol, which I wanted to understand. The cold and the loneliness, the wide road to perdition. I wanted to make a difference, to mean something to this forlorn individual, because I was in a friendly state of mind, and time was running out. I acquired another bottle of vodka and put it in the cupboard. And I continued to visit the park near Lake Mester. I sat on my bench and waited for the others; gradually they came trooping up, like beasts to a waterhole: Ebba, Lill Anita, Miranda, Eddie, and Janne. The huge unhappy black man from the Reception Center. The strange thing was, although Arnfinn and I could now be counted as friends, or at least acquaintances, he never seated himself next to me on my bench. And he never started a conversation when we met in the park. This was part of the ritual between us—that everything should be done in moderation. We both understood that. And we followed the unwritten rule that nothing should be too intimate, but remain in modest, decorous proportion. *Come to my house and drink yourself to warmth and brightness,* I thought, *but leave when the bottle's empty. I couldn't carry you the entire time; I had enough of my own black days.* So he was an unassuming friend in a mad world, a friend who kept me engaged and enthusiastic. It was something quite new in my barren and austere life.

I went to work. I watched Anna and all her doings closely. I pictured her aura: it was large and warm and red. I tried to enter it, but it wasn't easy. She was out of reach, as I'd always known she was. But I had something she wanted, something she lacked, something very valuable. The truth about her drowned brother Oscar. It was my great secret. But I kept it close, because I wanted it to last.

Waldemar Rommen passed away. No one was with him when he drew his last breath, but Dr. Fischer sat by his bed a long time mulling it over. The sad ending that overtakes us all. He was reminiscent of a mournful dog as he sat by the bed rubbing his temple. A few relatives eventually turned up to take their final farewell. One of them, a teenaged boy, seemed terrified by the thought of what lay in store. But there was nothing frightening about Waldemar. He lay like some ancient chieftain on his bed, with prominent cheekbones and a sharp, impressive nose. The undertakers took him away quite quickly, and we had an empty bed. A sixty-year-old woman with MS was admitted to the ward.

I paid a quick visit to the room to see to her. I had to assess her character and how I should behave toward her. She could speak, and she seemed orientated, so I couldn't do anything to her. I don't tempt providence.

Her name was Barbro Zanussi and she was in pain; every waking moment was torture to her. Each time I entered her room, she raised her head with extreme difficulty and looked me right in the eyes. It was a powerful, luminous look. As if she wished to transfer some of her suffering to me, and I must say she succeeded. Her husband, a small, dark Italian, came only once, and then with a set of divorce papers. Anna had to help her hold the pen, so that she could sign her name to their final separation.

The days and the weeks passed. The summer grew warmer, light and airy, and this was all the excuse people needed to go wild with joy. They threw off their clothes and went out, beguiled, their belief in life renewed. I frequently sat in the park by Lake Mester. I received Arnfinn; I listened, I filled up his hip flask. I went to work and plunged hypodermic syringes into mattresses and wrote nursing notes. I discussed things with Dr. Fischer and Sister Anna. Can we do anything for Barbro? asked Dr. Fischer with a tormented twist of his lips. No, we couldn't do a damned thing for Barbro. The disease took its course; it spread throughout her body with devastating effect. I went to the kitchen to see Sali Singh and gave him a friendly pat on the back. He gave no visible reaction to this touch; he was a simple man who lived in his own world. Maybe his mind was away in Delhi, in the slums he'd frequented as a boy. I could imagine Dr. Fischer as a young boy too, in shorts and patent leather shoes, and Anna in a blouse and pleated skirt. I had plenty of imagination. I watched them and thought my thoughts. Life was a gift, people said. Life was a challenge, a miracle, something God-given.

I wasn't so sure.

I saw so much toil and worry.

I heard so much moaning and misery.

Miranda's thin cheeks had begun to get a bit of color.

Old Ebba's bedspread had come on well; her hands worked rapidly, and the work grew in her lap from day to day. Eddie and

Janne were still together. They came at regular intervals and sat there fondling in the usual manner, always with the same greediness and intensity. I knew they spent some of their time at the Dixie Café, sucking Coke through a straw and ruining their teeth. We saw little of the black man now. Perhaps he'd been deported, or sent to another Reception Center. Maybe he'd found a job and some digs, but I thought it unlikely; I'd never been much of an optimist. I'd gotten used to Arnfinn fetching up at my door from time to time, begging for a treat like a child, just a wee drink. And I always let him in. There was something solid about him in spite of everything. Something straightforward and solid — yes, something unfeigned and honest and genuine. He always sat right in the corner of the sofa, bent slightly forward with his elbows on his knees. I told myself that he came for my company too; it wasn't only the vodka. He was like a great good-natured dog, sitting there holding his glass in both hands. And like a dog, he had that look; the look that says: Don't be cruel, I can't take all that much.

But the day came when I could no longer show such forbearance. My endurance had its limits too, and we breached them together, Arnfinn and I. It was a Friday in the middle of July, July 17, and I had the day off. Not because it was my birthday, which it was, but because I was due some time in lieu.

So it was July 17. Arnfinn came to my door that day. He stood hesitating on the bottom step with that mixture of embarrassment and shame I'd seen so often. Stooping forward with one hand on the handrail and imploring eyes. I'd become fond of this grave, somber man and his simple life, so I was pleased to see him. And I harbored a few pleasant thoughts about the future. The years would pass and Arnfinn would visit, as steadfast as the sun, to get his vodka.

He sat in the corner of the sofa as always. I fetched the bottle as usual, and immediately the conversation flowed more freely. He warmed to it so much that he sat and purred like a stove. I'd never been openhanded, but I watered him like a rare plant. In reality, I was teetering on a knife-edge; I just didn't realize it. Later in the afternoon, after the considerable quantity of vodka that I'd so generously poured for him, he headed to the toilet. It never occurred to me that everything was about to change. That everything would end in disaster and life would take a grisly twist from now on, his life and my life. Shortly afterward, he came out of the bathroom. He stood for a moment in the hallway, swaying. I could see him in the corner of my eye because I'd gotten up and gone to the window. But he hadn't realized this. He was standing there with something in his hand; he glanced quickly over his shoulder, a bowed and wary figure in the dimness of the hall. He'd picked up my wallet and was now turning it over. I usually left it on the sideboard once the bustle of the day was over. Of course he wasn't sober, so he took a couple of off-balance, sideways steps. Then the unthinkable happened. It felt like a slap in the face. Suddenly he opened my wallet and pulled out a couple of notes. They disappeared into his shirt pocket; it was all over in a matter of seconds.

Dear old Arnfinn. A man I'd thought of as a friend. With his grubby fingers deep inside my wallet.

In my consternation, I must have regurgitated some gastric juice, because I had a sour taste in my mouth, and the room began to spin in front of my eyes. Then he replaced my wallet on the sideboard. He walked back perfectly calmly and sat down in his sofa corner. I could see the bulge the notes made in his shirt pocket. But he sat there as if nothing had happened. Just as if he were still the same dear old Arnfinn.

My teeth were chattering with rage.

My arms were dangling like two clubs of solid stone.

"When I was little," Arnfinn began, in a voice that was exactly as normal because he didn't realize what was happening right in front of him. I was consumed with his treachery and my own fury; I was obsessed with the thought of the retribution I felt his mean theft deserved. "When I was little," he repeated, "there was a boy in my class; his name was Reidar. Was it Reidar? Yes. He wasn't quite all there, if you know what I mean. One day when his parents were out, he cut the legs off the family's budgie. With nail clippers. I was there, as a matter of fact, and I saw him do it. And I won't forget that legless budgie. It only weighed a few grams. A tiny ball of yellow feathers."

Here Arnfinn paused to fortify himself with vodka. Afterward he wiped his mouth on the back of his hand and coughed up a bit of mucus from his throat.

"When its legs came off," he went on, "it fell over on its side and died then and there. It was the shock, I should think. I remember the sound as the bird's small feet flicked through the air. There was a girl there too; she went into hysterics. Maybe she finds it difficult to sleep too," said Arnfinn. "We human beings find excuses for most things when it comes to justifying our actions. And the way we live. And all that stuff."

He took another gulp.

"Don't we, eh, Riktor? We find an excuse?"

He patted his shirt pocket. I suppose he wanted to make sure the money was still there. How much was it? I kept a couple of thousand kroner in cash, didn't I? Yes, I thought so, a couple of thousand of hard-earned money.

I couldn't utter a word. Rage gripped my heart and affected my circulation. I couldn't breathe. I felt powerless and white-faced, yet his words had conjured up a clear image of the legless bird, although the story was probably a lie. Just as the story about the snake would have been a lie. The way Arnfinn's whole person was one big lie, a drunken bluff. A coarse felon, a deceiver. I'd thoroughly misjudged him; it was more than I could bear. *I opened my door to you,* I reflected bitterly. *I poured vodka for you. I replenished your hip flask every single time.*

He gazed a little uncertainly at me as I crossed the floor. Perhaps he caught something in my manner, something new and ominous, for he was suddenly on his guard.

"Aren't you feeling well?" he asked. "You look very pale."

I walked past him without a word.

Across the room, past the sofa, and into the kitchen, propelled by something so explosive that I struggled to control my pulse and breathing. I had some tools in a drawer, including a large hammer. It had a rubber grip and felt comfortable in the hand. With the hammer raised, I went back into the living room. I was no longer bereft of power; I was mad with anger. He knew nothing about what happened next. The vodka had made him slow, and I was as quick as a rattlesnake. The last thing I saw was his eyes, a surprised expression, and a movement as if he wanted to get up and leave. Leave the house and go down the road, with my money in his pocket.

Arnfinn the thief. Arnfinn the traitor, the deceiver, the drunk, the sponger, and the parasite. The head of the hammer struck home. I hit him once with all my strength; it felt like cracking a huge egg. He fell over onto his side and then rolled onto the floor. The hammer had left a great dent in his skull. I heard a feeble moaning. It was coming from the depths of his lungs and didn't sound quite human. I was terribly disturbed by this moaning. It seemed to penetrate the very marrow of my bones, and now there was no way back. I had to strike again. I had to make him cease his noise once and for all. But it felt impossible. I no longer had that fire inside me; my fury had dissipated, but a corner of my brain worked feverishly on the problem. None of my neighbors could see the rear of my house. If I waited until dark, I could dig a grave on the edge of the forest bordering my back garden and push him into it. I could manage perfectly well without lights, and no one ever came to the door, certainly not at night. I was gripping the hammer. Now it felt as heavy as lead. I had a cramp in my fingers and the rubberized shaft felt hot in my hand. I paced the floor and thought about what I'd just done—the gravity of it, that I'd smashed a man's skull. Everything had happened so fast; I'd had no time to think. My God, I'd struck him in a blind rage. I began to walk around and around while Arnfinn lay there whimpering.

I'd have to hit him again.

But at that moment, at that very instant, as I stood with the hammer raised and lined up above Arnfinn's head, there was a ring at the door. I started like a thief. Nobody ever came to the house, and this was hardly a convenient moment.

The hammer suddenly felt out of place in my hand, as if put there by something outside myself, an alien force. Obviously I couldn't open the door. Presumably it was just a salesman, or someone collecting for famine relief in Africa. Or cancer research, or the blind; so many people come begging. So I stood in the middle of the room holding the hammer and waiting, as if frozen fast by my own evil deed. I listened and counted the seconds. There was another strident ring. Then I heard an alarming sound. I nearly lost my composure altogether when I realized what was happening. Someone was turning the handle of the door and opening it. And I remembered that the door wasn't locked; I hadn't turned the key again after Arnfinn had arrived.

Now someone had opened it.

And that someone was at this very moment standing on the doorstep.

"Riktor? Are you there?"

Then silence for a couple of seconds. There was the sound of light footsteps.

"It's only me. Are you at home? May I come in?"

I recognized the voice at once. Sister Anna was standing out there calling; she was the one trying to get in—angel Anna, that good fairy, suddenly here in my house. And here I was, clutching a blood-covered hammer. A miserable alcoholic was lying on the floor with his skull smashed in. A dying man. A moaning man. I laid the hammer on the floor and carefully studied my hands. I couldn't see any blood on them. I stepped over Arnfinn and crossed the room quickly and went out into the hall. Anna was standing with one foot on the doorstep. She was holding a plate with a small cake on it.

"Many happy returns!" she said, brightening as I made my appearance. "I know you're off duty. But you'll have to put up with a little interruption on your birthday."

I was overwhelmed by everything about her. The red dress she wore, the walnut–topped marzipan cake she held in her hands.

"Happy birthday," she said again. And then, with a light laugh: "Have I caught you in the midst of some evil deed?"

I could only stand there and gawk. I couldn't utter a word. My heart almost stopped and I felt boiling hot.

"Maybe you've got a female visitor?" Anna asked.

The question fazed me completely. I was about to nod, yes, I had, just to gain time, when a deep groan from the living room echoed through the house, and out to the door where we stood. Anna immediately became solemn. The cake dish tilted in her hand. She took a small step back and bit her lip, her eyes big with surprise.

"You've got someone with you," she said uncertainly.

72

"It's my father," I replied. I said it quickly and without thinking. "He's poorly," I added, "so he's staying here a few days. Because he's ill. He's pretty frail," I went on. "He calls out whenever I disappear from view."

I could have bitten my tongue off. I was beginning to get slightly manic, and I still hadn't taken the cake.

"Your father?" Anna said doubtfully. Then she slowly shook her head. "Your father?" she repeated skeptically.

"I'm rather busy," I said clumsily. "Or I'd ask you in. For a cup of coffee. But there's my father. He's lying on the sofa in the living room. So it's a bit inconvenient."

She sent me a look of incomprehension and shook her head almost imperceptibly, as if there was something she didn't understand. She turned and glanced over her shoulder, as if searching for an answer somewhere on the driveway. I could see that she was struggling to make sense of the situation. Then she held out the cake and nodded.

"I see," she said. "Your father. Well, I'm sorry to hear he's poorly. You must share the cake with him."

I took the dish and thanked her. Anna retreated to the top of the steps. She stood there for a moment or two, as if considering. And I thought to myself, if Arnfinn moans again, it'll all be over. Or perhaps it was all over anyway, because the excuse about my father had been a bit rash. Vague recollections of previous conversations, chats when we'd been sitting in the ward office, for example, had begun to plague my mind. What I'd revealed and hadn't revealed over the years.

"I'm sorry I took the liberty," Anna said, "of opening the door and coming in. But I was so certain you were in the house. You always say it yourself, how you like being at home."

I couldn't come up with any answer. I was still paralyzed with

73

fear at the idea that Arnfinn might groan again. But he didn't; there was no sound from the living room. I made a bow as I stood in the doorway, with the cake dish in my hands.

"Thank you for the kind thought," I said, as effusively as I could. "You're in a league of your own when it comes to birthdays."

"I think you ought to go back in to your father," she said emphatically. "When someone makes that sort of noise, it must be serious."

Then she turned on her heel. She jogged down the steps and onto the driveway. I caught a glimpse of her car parked by the gate. Afterward I was totally bewildered. I could hardly believe what had happened; perhaps it was no more than a bad dream. And as I stood there like an idiot with the cake dish in my hands something reignited my fury, as if a spring within me was wound to the breaking point. I slammed the front door shut behind me, dumped the cake on the sideboard, and ran into the living room. I picked up the hammer from the floor and stood there, legs apart, an enraged crook in my knees, seeing the prostrate Arnfinn through the red mist that hung before my eyes.

Then I began to lash out.

I pounded for a good while, the blows landing somewhat randomly on his head and face, and also on his chest, my fury fuelling my strength. I'd never been so savage and demented. I kept going until I was totally exhausted. I stood staring down at his gory, pulped head. I could no longer tell that it was Arnfinn lying there. A gray and porridge-like substance had poured out of his nose. The membrane around his brain had ruptured. The contents were flowing out, running over his lips and chin.

17

AFTERWARD, WHEN MY equilibrium had returned, I cut a slice of cake, put it on a plate, and carried it into the living room. I sat and ate while I contemplated the object that lay on the floor. The cake was topped with pale green marzipan and filled with raspberries and cream. The slice had a walnut perched on the icing.

I'd killed a man.

I'd killed him because of a few banknotes, killed him because I'd been hurt. I'd shattered his skull because I'd been taken in and deceived. I was indignant. It was Arnfinn who'd gotten me into this predicament. Now he'd turned into an insurmountable obstacle, as he lay on the floor with the contents of his brain oozing out over the floorboards and seeping into them. I finished my slice of cake. I saved the walnut until last. I tramped around the house swearing. I cursed him and hurled imprecations at him, against the drunkard, the thief, the deceiver. I had a long night before me. It's not easy to dispose of a man's body; Arnfinn was hardly something you could just flush down the toilet. But oh, what a wonderful solution, if only it had been that easy! He deserved no more, even though at certain moments of generosity I hadn't realized it; I had seen him as a sterling character, a modest creature. My next thought, as I walked around with my hands pressed to my head, was that no one would miss him. But it would be the same when my own time came; not a living soul would regret my passing. When my tough, old heart muscle had contracted for the last time.

I waited until darkness had fallen late that night before going to work. In the cellar, I found a spade and immediately set to work, digging with hard, desperate thrusts, just on the edge of the forest. It was harder than I'd imagined. I'd never had much of a physique; the intellect was more my métier. The blade only bit a few centimeters into the hard, dry ground, and I quickly realized that I'd never manage to dig a grave two meters deep. At best I'd be able to scoop out a shallow trench. I'd have to pile earth on the body and cover it as best I could. Nobody ever came to the house, so nobody would see the small mound in among the pines and birches. Nobody would think there was anything mysterious about an inconspicuous pile of stones on the brow of the forest. So I dug; my God, how I dug. There was a crisp, slicing sound each time the blade cut into the sandy soil. There were also a lot of stones and several roots that caused big problems. All of this began to infuriate me. With the anger came adrenaline, and that provided more strength, which I badly needed in order to conceal my unfortunate accident. I looked around and wiped away the sweat.

If it had been November, the darkness would have shrouded me and my evil deeds. But the summer night was transparent, and I prayed that my neighbors were asleep. The noise of digging carried far on the still air, and with each thrust I moaned a little as much from exertion as rising panic. Now and then I rested on my spade. I panted and wiped away the sweat and then thought about Arnfinn lying in the living room. I had a lot of cleaning up to do as well. Much of the contents of Arnfinn's head had spilled over the floorboards and run down the cracks, and that might have implications. I'll have to do it a bit at a time, I thought. I drove the spade into the ground; again and again I drove it into the soil, urged on by rage and despair. Why the hell did this have to happen! Those blows that had worked the fury out of my body had been satisfying and wholly necessary, but I could well have done without all this cleaning up. I took a breather. Suddenly I saw a cat slinking in from the forest; it watched me from among the trees, paused for a few seconds, and then padded off. It felt strange being stared at. Even if it was only by a cat with yellow eyes: an intense, unblinking gaze. I went on digging. The spade continued to strike roots and stones, and the impact sent jarring pains up my arm. But the whole situation seemed familiar too. As if it were something I'd always known, that this was how it would end. As if my life had been mapped out in advance, and that I, in a few brief glimpses, had discerned the outline of the crime to come. That this was why I lay awake at night. And why there was so much din in the room from the diesel engine.

All this went through my mind as I dug.

I worked as hard as I could, but after an hour I'd only made a shallow trench in the ground, two meters long. It might have been deep enough to bury a broom handle, or perhaps in a pinch, little Miranda. But she wasn't the one I'd killed. So I went on digging. I drove the spade into the earth with all my might and scraped, hacked, and pounded with the sharp tip. The sound carried in the silence. Each time the spade struck a stone, there was a loud ringing clang. Come and see, come and see, look what Riktor's done, murder! Would there ever be enough room for Arnfinn in this grave, I wondered, as I toiled on. I worked up more rage, more despair, more desperation. And then at last it was as if I'd passed over some threshold. All at once everything became so easy, and I had the strength of a lion. I dug; I was completely unstoppable.

Finally the grave was finished. I leaned heavily on my spade. I felt like a proper workman, someone who gets things done.

Later on, when I had to haul the heavy corpse out of the living room, the weight of it was almost too much. Never had a man been so heavy. I had to pause repeatedly for breath. His head, or what was left of it, thudded against the treads going down the steps, but I paid no heed to that. I just wanted to get him buried. Once on the gravel, I dragged him around the back of the house through the grass and over to the yawning grave. I peered into its black earthiness. One day I, too, would lie in a hole in the ground. But there'd be no one to take care of things when that day arrived. Only a few bored council workers, perhaps. The ceremony would fall on deaf ears. Suddenly I felt deeply depressed at the idea of my own impending death. And, no matter how much I tried, it was impossible to lay Arnfinn neatly on his back in the grave, with his hands folded across his stomach, as I'd originally intended. I shoved him over the edge, and he fell heavily into the hole, face down. He was squashed up against the wall of earth. His legs were splayed and his arms were beneath him; it wasn't a pretty sight. *Not very restful,* I thought, straightening my back. It was quiet; there were no sounds from the neighboring houses. But people might have heard the noise of the spade in the stillness. And later on they'd remember that there'd been some digging over at Riktor's house. On the night of July 17. Yes, we heard it clearly; we heard a spade striking against rock. They'd mention it to the police, who'd doubtless go from door to door to find out what had happened to the lonely alcoholic from the park by Lake Mester. As far as I knew, nobody was aware of my association with Arnfinn, but you never could tell. When it came to the police, it was a mistake to underestimate them. Even the force had its share of smart cookies. What I could rely on with confidence was my ability to lie with complete conviction. I could look people straight in the eye and lie without blinking, and they would nod and believe what I said. It was easy. I began shoveling earth over the corpse. Well, Arnfinn, I thought, this isn't quite what you were expecting, but it's more than Anna's brother got. He's rotting on the bottom of Lake Mester.

I spent more than an hour cleaning up.

That night I lay awake.

I could still feel Arnfinn's proximity outside the house, as if some heat remained in his body, something smoldering slowly out there on the edge of the forest, like the embers in a hearth. For a long while, I mused on Arnfinn and his weak character. The sort of man who gnaws away at people—like some carnivorous bacterium, I thought—who didn't deserve to die perhaps, but who'd overstepped the mark with such audacity that it took my breath away.

And then my reason.

At the same time, there was something nagging at a corner of my mind, a feeling that I'd overlooked something important, something incriminating. I knew the police would arrive; I wasn't naive. Two men presumably, I surmised, standing on the steps in their dark uniforms, legs apart. Two detached and dependable men who'd require an explanation for the sounds of digging. I could do nothing but await the hour of reckoning. I drew up my knees and lay with my hands clamped between my thighs, like a frightened child, and waited for sleep. Trying all the while to suss out the feeling, the anxiety, that I'd made a mistake. As if beating Arnfinn to death hadn't been a mistake. Just think how Anna had come to the door, and with a delicious cake as well. What did it mean? Only that she's considerate, I said, scolding myself as I lay in bed. If only I had a woman! My elbows ached after the digging. If anyone came to the house, if anyone took the trouble to look around the back, they'd immediately notice the small mound of earth, so I was hoping for rain. I was hoping for a shower that would settle the earth and make it appear more natural. At last, I couldn't be bothered to lie there sleepless anymore, so I got up, slipped on a dressing gown, and went out of the house. Around the corner, through the grass, and over to the grave. Despondency overtook me and I stood staring, dry-eyed. I can explain, I mumbled to myself, if you'll both just listen. I turned and went into the house again and stood looking out of the window. A car passed slowly with its lights on. I followed the circles of light through the darkness and took the car as an omen. That someone was keeping me under surveillance. I laid my forehead against the windowpane. It's madness, I whispered into the darkness—everything in this world, everything we human beings did to one another. The pious will also perish, and we'll get no reward in heaven. So what was the point of exerting ourselves?

18

I got up and went to work, quite determined to boast about Sister Anna's cake. I enjoyed imagining the cake as a declaration of love, even though I knew it was nothing of the kind. I did possess some self-awareness, but a lovely daydream was not to be shunned. It was a gray day with threatening clouds, and I wished that rain would come and wash away all traces of the night's misdeeds, that luck would be on my side. Why shouldn't it be? Arnfinn, I hoped, would be able to rest there in perpetuity, on the edge of the forest. And become a part of the great cycle of life, without anyone knowing. Just as Anna's brother lay at rest on the bottom of Lake Mester, undisturbed by the living. As if nature can't deal with things herself, without any help from us. She devours us and converts us, and other living organisms feed on us. It's really a lovely thought. But when I bumped into Anna in the corridor, I could see right away that there was something on her mind. That there was something she was puzzling over. That's the strange thing about a person's eyes, how much they can express, the colored iris against the white background, and the black pupil pulsating. The delicate lines in the corner of the eye. A set of highly tuned messages that can broadcast displeasure, skepticism, or joy in a fraction of a second.

I latch on to such things instantly.

And Anna had a message. So I avoided her for as long as possible; I kept away from the ward office and paced the corridors instead. Then she suddenly emerged from Barbro's room. I stepped aside to let her pass, but she stopped, stretched out a hand, and plucked at my coat.

"Your father's dead," she said.

I drew a deep breath and let it out again.

"What are you talking about?" I asked. "Why are you bringing that up?"

"He's dead," she repeated. "You sat there in the ward office and told everyone about it, that he died of a massive thrombosis when you were fourteen. So how could he have been lying on your sofa groaning?"

My mind worked like lightning. Had I really told them that, about my father dying? I couldn't remember. But she was right, of course; we did talk about that sort of thing, and everyone knew that my parents were dead. I gave her my widest smile and patted her gently on the arm.

"Oh, that!" I said, with a glint in my eye. "Of course he's dead. He died years ago. It was only a little white lie; one has to tell them sometimes."

"Well?" she said. "And so?"

"An old friend paid me a visit yesterday and, regrettably, we had a slight altercation. So I bashed him on the head with a hammer. It was probably him you heard. He was stretched out on the floor wailing like a baby."

Anna shook her head in despair.

"I'll never understand you," she said. "No one on the ward will ever understand you."

She started to walk away but then changed her mind and gave me a penetrating look.

"But what happened to your acquaintance? After you bashed him on the head?"

"Oh, he went and died," I said. "And now he's buried behind the house. I had quite a busy night of it, I can tell you. I was digging for hours. I was totally wiped out."

Another sigh of resignation. Then she strode off down the corridor. I could see that she'd brushed it all aside, all the nonsense that had spouted from my mouth. Because other things had entered her thoughts. She had her brother to think about; they still hadn't found him. And there were plenty of patients on our ward. Several were close to death.

I went to the park near Lake Mester after my shift.

I sat there looking at Arnfinn's bench, and melancholy thoughts began to assail my mind, about how he was gone forever and nobody knew it. The murder was with me every moment. It was in my head and in my heart, and in the hand that had raised the hammer. And welling up was the realization that I really had done it, not merely dreamed it.

Because he'd driven me to the breaking point.

The park was quiet except for a few hopping sparrows. Perhaps they found the odd crumb; at any rate they searched energetically, and watching them soothed me. Ebba didn't come, nor did Lill Anita and Miranda. Maybe the large black man had found work at last. Wouldn't that be something, I thought, if someone had finally discovered that mound of muscle. I sat on the bench and brooded on the murder. I felt deeply irritated that Arnfinn had been such a fool. He'd finally found a source, a wellspring of vodka, and in an instant he'd thrown it all away. Drops began to fall from the sky. Lightly at first, then heavily, until it was a constant, calming swish. I looked on it as a portent, that nature was on my side, because now the little barrow of earth at the back of the house would settle and blend with the landscape. And Arn-finn would, quite literally, become part of nature. I sat out in the rain for a good while. I sat and mulled over this new twist to my life, and marveled at it all—at the way his deceit could push me over the edge like that. It had happened so quickly that I hadn't had time to think. At last, I was soaked to the skin; the July rain was mild, so it wasn't that I was cold, but I just couldn't relax. Every now and again my crime would surface in all its horror and make my ears burn.

19

THE FIRST TIME he arrived was on July 27. My heart thudded wildly as I stood on the steps, staring down at him. The police so soon—I'd hardly gotten back on an even keel. And what with Arnfinn buried behind the house, it was insupportable. But there he was, and I was finding it difficult to breathe. My pulse was racing and I was gasping for air. My hands were cold and shriveled. I hadn't expected things to move so fast. It was only ten days since the murder—the fatal event that was to propel my life in a new and miserable direction. I'd been naive, that was the problem. I'd imagined that the wheels would turn more slowly. Of course they'd eventually come to the door; they'd eventually trace Arnfinn all the way from the park to my small red house at Jordahl. People had seen us, damn them. There were eyes and ears everywhere, I thought.

"Randers," he said. "Police."

I stammered out a few polite phrases. He gave me a quick nod. Just then a shudder ran through my body, all the way from my head to my feet. I stood gawking in the doorway. I was unable to utter a word, as my thoughts were in disarray. Randers nudged gravel into a little heap with his toe. He was dressed in jeans and a leather jacket; his appearance was impeccably masculine. He was about my age, but much better looking of course. All men were better looking than me. It wasn't difficult; I was the dregs in every conceivable sense. And he'd already managed, by some means I didn't comprehend, to find his way to my house.

But even though Arnfinn's grave was only a few meters away, I managed to raise my head and look him in the eye. No one can lie like I could. No one could mislead with such consummate plausibility. These were the talents I fell back on as I stood on the doorstep gazing down on the law.

"May I come in?"

I hesitated for a moment or two. If he wanted to enter the house, it must mean that his questions wouldn't simply be trivial or routine. Something more, something that took time, some evidence, or chance witness statements, perhaps from people who frequented the park. Or from people who'd seen Arnfinn near my house. But if I refused, it would look suspicious; so I retreated obligingly into the hallway and motioned him in. Randers mounted the steps. He was tall, perhaps one meter ninety, clean-shaven, and neat. A masculine scent of aftershave hung in the air after him.

I felt not a shadow of doubt. He was in a class of his own.

"Randers," I remarked courteously. "Like the town in Denmark?"

He smiled, but only fleetingly. He moved into the living room and glanced around it, walking in a way that was so confoundedly self-assured that it made me nervous. Just keep calm, I said to myself. Everything has to be proved, with no room for doubt. Internally I sent furious commands to my heart to slow down, but it wouldn't be appeased. It was pounding so hard that I was certain it must be audible as a distant thunder, saying "guilty, guilty." This admission, coursing through my head, was making me blush. Such were my thoughts as Randers drank in the room. My old, gray corner sofa where Arnfinn had sat, the computer on the desk, the Advent star in the window.

"You live alone?" Randers asked.

His voice had power. The voice of a man with weight and authority, I mused, and nodded.

"Yes," I said, "alone. I've always lived here by myself."

He sat down on the sofa, unbidden. He sat in exactly the same place as Arnfinn, right in the corner. He arranged his long legs and leaned forward slightly.

"Nice house," he declared. "Secluded. Pleasant view."

I agreed and took a chair. And so we sat for several long seconds looking at each other. I disliked the silence; it was oppressive. I felt as if I were an open book, and Randers's brow was furrowed.

"I come into contact with lots of people," he went on. "And I see how they live. It's interesting. I mean, the way we want to appear to others. Riktor," he added. "An authoritative name. Your father's choice?"

"My mother's," I answered tersely.

"I think that a house says a lot about its owner. The things we surround ourselves with. There isn't much lying around in here. It's very tidy."

"I always keep it that way," I replied. "Mess has a habit of migrating to the brain, and there's enough litter up there as it is. I can't stand untidiness. It shows a lack of discipline."

He considered what I'd just said.

"And you're concerned about discipline?" Again he flashed his quick smile.

"Naturally," I replied.

He kept quiet again for some time. I sat waiting politely. It was evident that he had plenty of time, ensconced as he was in the corner of the sofa.

"You're a nurse?" he asked at length.

I nodded. I crossed one leg over the other and kept calm. I relaxed my shoulders and raised my chin, because I know that body language is important. So he realized that I worked as a nurse. But the fact that he'd already made a number of inquiries wasn't disquieting in itself. I'd been expecting that.

"It must be demanding," he hazarded. "Having to attend to other people's needs the whole time."

I took my time replying. It was important to maintain composure; he mustn't be allowed to push me over the edge.

"Let me put it this way: you develop a special attitude to death."

"How so?" he inquired.

"Because it happens all the time. The patients I look after are frail and elderly. And, if you'll forgive me using a crude, if accurate, expression, they drop like flies."

"Well, that's one way of putting it," he said, a smile on his lips. "But presumably with old people there isn't a lot of drama about it. Am I right?"

"Some of them simply die in their sleep," I said. "We hardly notice their passing; so yes, to a certain extent, of course you're right. But there are always exceptions. Some of them cough up a bit of blood. And some fight, struggling against the inevitable."

"A death agony, you mean?"

"Yes. It's more common than people think. And it's something you never forget, once you've witnessed it."

"D'you like it?" he asked bluntly.

"I beg your pardon?"

"Let's not beat around the bush here," Randers said. "You deal with death on a daily basis, just as I do. So between ourselves:

there are certain reasons for our choice of job. You're attracted to the drama of the situation, isn't that right?"

"It makes an impression," I replied. "It certainly does make an impression. That'll have to do for an answer."

I was trying to work out where the conversation was leading. But talking about my job felt safe, so I answered his questions willingly.

"You must have a special relationship with death and decay as well," I said. "I mean, because of what you do."

The fleeting smile came and went.

"Yes, I've seen most things. Some of it's horrifying, and I never get used to it. There are certain details I could well do without. But I won't rehearse them for you. You've probably got enough horror stories of your own."

He sat studying my face. As if the crime might be visible there, as a particular gleam in the eyes perhaps. He looked at my hands as if they might be stained black, those guilty hands. But the killing was done and justified; it was more like dregs at the bottom of a bottle. There was silence as we sat sizing each other up. He was wearing an insufferable grin, as if there were lots of things he knew, while I went delving into hundreds of ideas searching for an explanation.

"So now you're going from door to door?" I inquired lightly.

Randers stretched an arm along the back of the sofa. "No, not from door to door," he said. "I'm only calling on you today."

His smile widened.

"Aren't you going to ask why I'm here?"

I sat up in my chair. His comment caught me slightly unawares.

"Naturally. Obviously you're here for some reason."

"If the police arrived at my door, I would have asked right away," he said. "Asked them why they were there."

"Well, yes, I'm on tenterhooks," I said, inwardly cursing my slowness, for not thinking of that, for not thinking to ask what he wanted.

"We believe there's the possibility of a suspicious death," he said gravely.

I looked at him for a good, long while. Weighing every word.

"A suspicious death. Believe? You're not certain? Have you come just to check, to make sure a crime *hasn't* been committed? In which case, it's rather a relief; I can relax a bit. Carry on, I'm all ears."

Once again he waited a long time. The silence was filled with noise from inside my own head, where my thoughts were in tumult.

"We call it reasonable grounds for suspicion," he said. "Just now we're seeing how the land lies. You're an obvious candidate for questioning."

"Why?"

Randers leaned forward again.

"There appears to be a clear connection between you and the victim. What people have seen, events, and other details. We've got plenty of time. We've begun an investigation, and it will keep ticking over until everything's cleared up."

"I live on my own," I put in. "Well, I only want to mention it because it's relevant. My connections to other people are extremely limited. So I find what you're saying pretty incomprehensible."

Randers stretched his legs. He was wearing expensive shoes with leather laces.

"Everyone has connections to someone," he declared. "And you're no exception."

"Yes," I retorted. "I am an exception. But you don't realize it, because it's part of your job to believe that all people have things in common. I don't wish to sound arrogant, but I'm really not much like other people."

"What do you do in your spare time? If you don't have anything to do with people."

"I often go to the park near Lake Mester. I sit by the fountain and ponder life."

"And death," Randers interjected. "You ponder death as well, no doubt. Isn't it a part of your work?"

"Yes, that's true, I often ponder death. But I know nothing about what you call a suspicious death." I shrugged my shoulders. "So I'm sorry. You'll just have to find another door."

Randers held my gaze. And even though I could take quite a lot, I was extremely nervous.

"Often the motives for murder are trivial," Randers explained. "And that's our theory about this crime."

"You don't know that," I said. "It's merely an assumption."

"Correct, an assumption. Because that's what my experience tells me. We've got some clues as well, important leads. We can return to that; we've time enough. What are you like, Riktor? Get on well with people?"

"No," I admitted, "not especially. That's why I keep away from them. But I like superficial contact of the sort I can strike up with patients on the ward. They haven't long to go, after all."

Randers rose from the sofa. He crossed to the window and stood gazing through it.

"Do you often stand here looking out?"

"I do. And people pass by. They cycle, or they run. Some push carriages, some have dogs. I like making up stories about them," I said, "where they're going to, why they're running, what they're running from, why they wanted that child, if they regret things perhaps, regret all those choices that can't be undone. It gives me a feeling of control. And it's important for me to have control. There. Now you've got some data for your perpetrator profile."

He gave a short laugh. He turned and went back to the sofa, seating himself in the corner.

"Who's the victim?" I asked innocently.

"Ah," he prevaricated. "I thought you'd never ask. Not one of the pillars of society, perhaps," he confessed. "But still, a life is a life."

Half an hour later, he got into a green Volvo and turned out onto the road. I could hear him changing gear. He'd quizzed me about my professional career and my childhood and youth. I'd told him the truth, that I lived alone, and always have. I didn't say anything about women. That a woman was what I wanted more than anything in the world. He probably had several: a wife, almost certainly, and a mistress or two as well. He was certainly macho enough for it. And they were sure to be beautiful too, if not as beautiful as Anna Otterlei.

I brushed him away like so much dust. I put on some warm clothes and went to the park by Lake Mester and sat there mulling over the conversation we'd had. I'd done reasonably well, I thought, all things considered. Ebba was sitting with her crocheting. She plied her needle rapidly. She had a long length in her lap, big, six-pointed stars within a border.

"It soothes my mind," she explained.

We didn't usually converse. But she wanted to say a few words, so I listened politely, because that's the sort of person I was. I humored people and fit in with them, so they would remain at a safe distance.

"You know," she went on, "thoughts follow a pattern, just like my needle. They run in the same grooves every day. And they get deeper the more you think. In the end, you can't see over the edge. Then you end up like one of those rats in a maze. A fat rat," she said and laughed.

The needle glinted between her fingers.

"But if you do something with your hands, your thoughts are eased and they find new paths."

I nodded.

"We certainly weren't meant to sit doing nothing, that's for sure," she declared. "It's not good for the mind. But maybe you haven't got problems like that?" she asked, looking up. "From what I can see, you're a serene man."

She worked in silence for a while. When I made no reply, she continued: "I've crocheted bedspreads for years, and I never tire of it. I raffle them at Women's Voluntary Association bazaars. They make excellent prizes. A handmade bedspread like this costs several thousand kroner in the shops, and I could have made a bit of money out of all this work. But then, I'm frightened some of the pleasure would disappear. If I did it for profit, I mean. What do you think?" she inquired, raising her eyes again. "Would some of the pleasure disappear?"

"Making money is an excellent motivator," I said. "And we human beings aren't a noble race to begin with. Greed is everywhere and permeates everything, that's my opinion."

Ebba lowered her crocheting and became pensive.

"Oh, but there are so many exceptions," she exclaimed. "Look at that young mother who comes here, the one with the little girl in the wheelchair. She'll have to push that wheelchair around all her life. Because it's her duty. But she never complains. Isn't there something noble in that?"

"We really don't know how much she complains," I put in. "She won't do it when strangers are present. Anyway, I know a lot about this business of complaining. I work with the sick and elderly up at Løkka. They've all got something wrong with them and, I can assure you, they complain all right."

She took hold of her crocheting again. I looked at the long white length. There must have been millions of stitches in a bedspread like that when it was complete. Millions.

"Well, well. You're a good Samaritan; it warms my old heart to hear it. People suffer a lot, you know. The elderly gentleman who comes here, the one who drinks, he probably doesn't have an easy time of it. Actually, I haven't seen him for a while, but he's sure to turn up again."

"Of course he has an easy time," I objected. "His life just revolves around that bottle. When he isn't drinking, he's probably asleep. That's a simple enough life."

"Hm, well," Ebba replied. "But take those two doves. I mean, the two youngsters who often sit on each other's laps on the bench." She nodded to the place where Eddie and Janne usually sat groping. "They're both so unsullied. They're growing up in the finest country in the world. They can do whatever they want in life, and they certainly don't want each other for money's sake. It can't get much better than that, wouldn't you agree?"

"Oh, just you wait," I answered. "They'll both become bitter and fickle in a few years' time. Once Janne meets a man with more money."

"You're so hard on people," she said, crocheting away for all she was worth. "And you oughtn't to be, you're a real gentleman."

"I've got a protruding jaw," I said, "and my eyes are the color of cod liver oil. My life's not easy, I can tell you."

She gave a hearty laugh. Her teeth were white and perfect, despite her age.

"You're hard on yourself too," she said. "Don't be. We're only here for a short while. Tomorrow we'll probably all be gone. I don't mean literally, but we're only a heartbeat away from eternity. Then we won't be here anymore—think of that. Yes, just think of it!"

She lowered her crocheting again.

"We need to feel valued, that's important. Think of that huge man from the Refugee Reception Center who sits here sometimes; you must have seen him. He's lost his sense of self-esteem because no one wants him. It's all over then; I think about it often. Sometimes I've felt like saying a few friendly words to him, but he's so big. If you know what I mean. It's almost as if I don't want him to notice me. I don't dare arouse all that power. Did you know that he talks to himself?"

"No," I said.

"It might mean that he's psychotic," Ebba said. "And you mustn't take any chances with them. Or what do you think?"

20

I WENT TO work.

I was on the late shift and was on duty until eight. It was a quiet day on the ward. Only the occasional moan was heard from behind closed doors, like a distant lament. All that lamentation. I paced the corridors and thought of that policeman, Randers, and my imagination ran riot. It was as if Arnfinn's murder had a peculiar, unholy energy, and now it clung to my whole being like a special smell. That was probably why I saw nothing of the others. They can smell it, I thought, and they flee. Eventually I found Sali Singh in the kitchen. To my amazement, he was sitting at the table eating. Not the stuff he'd made himself, but some kind of ready meal he must have heated in the microwave.

"I didn't know you went in for this sort of thing," I said, sitting down next to him.

He went on slurping. It looked like soup with bits of fish in it.

"I am celebrating," he said. "This is a fine day."

I put my elbows on the table.

"What are you celebrating? Is it your birthday?"

He shook his ponderous head.

"I won at the Øvrevoll races," he said. "One hundred and forty thousand kroner. Just this Sunday."

I was dumbfounded.

"At Øvrevoll? You bet on the horses?"

He pushed the bowl of fish soup away and nodded.

"Suddenly they all came in. And I have been betting for years, so it was about time. My heart has never pounded so hard," he said, laying a golden-brown hand on his chest. "Not even when I proposed to my wife."

"What are you going to do with the money?"

He shrugged his shoulders.

"For now, I will keep it. In an account. And it can stay there just for show. But I shall greet it every day; I will call the bank and ask after it. I will watch over it as if it was a holy cow. You do not know of what we Indians are capable."

"Where is everyone?" I inquired. "Sister Anna and Dr. Fischer?"

"They are in with Barbro. She has been screaming all day." He cupped a hand behind his ear and listened. "Yes, she is screaming still," he added. "It is impossible for a person to scream like that; I feel that I want to go home almost. But when I am at home, I still hear her, in my thoughts. And she will lie screaming until she dies. Dr. Fischer is in despair. He cannot do her medication; nothing seems to work. So now he has consulted a doctor at the National Hospital in Oslo."

Sali leaned across the table. There was a peculiar intensity in his brown eyes.

"But the bitter truth, Riktor, is that not everyone can be helped. And I hope the gods will put me in the right category. I mean, when my turn comes."

I glanced across the table at Sali, that plump, likeable man, dressed in something that resembled a pair of blue pajamas. So he had a secret passion for the turf, who would have believed it? To be honest, I didn't like it, the fact that I'd overlooked this trait in him. Because I liked to think that I understood people and knew who they were. The way I knew Dr. Fischer and understood his ambitions and his frustration when he could only help a bit, or not at all, as in Barbro's case. He could hardly know that the only things she was getting from me were Tic Tacs and vitamins.

After my conversation with Sali, I went down to the mortuary. It was Løkka's small chapel for the dead, with a bier, a little table, and a candle. A lace tablecloth, a Bible, and a cross high up on the wall, made of brass.

I was often drawn to this room in the basement. I liked being alone here in the dimly lit room, even when it was empty, as it was now. But often it was occupied by someone waiting to be collected by the undertaker, and I relished that special feeling of being in the company of the dead. To study the sunken eyes and the blue lips. The hands that were soon covered with black marks, the mouth that slid open. On a few occasions, I had, just for amusement's sake, bent over the departed making horrible faces. Thumbs in my ears, tongue sticking out. Purely because I couldn't stop myself. Now, an idea came to me, an impulse that had to be instantly obeyed. I got up and lay flat on the vacant bier. My hands clasped over my stomach, eyes closed. I breathed quietly, felt my chest rise and fall, felt the joy of being alive, in my forties, still relatively young. That I could still play a practical joke or two. But what if someone came in right now, I mused, and came across me playing dead? The thought of the possible consequences sent me into raptures. Anna would hide her face in her hands; Dr. Fischer would slump against the wall. I jumped down and went back to the ward, where a strange stillness reigned. Barbro had been given fentanyl; at last she'd stopped screaming.

There was something in the air.

It couldn't be ignored. It was something indefinable, an alien note, like the humming in a cable or a sudden vibration. And I thought of the people I worked with, and how their looks had assumed an evasive quality. They lowered their eyes or turned them away; there was a special glint of suspicion. I was highly sensitive to such things. I opened my hands and examined my palms, but I couldn't see the murder, the evil intent, the fury I'd felt toward Arnfinn. I could see no guilt in the fine creases. My hands were quite clean and my heart beat softly. There was no remorse, only astonishment. At the way it had happened so quickly, at the way nothing could have stopped me from boiling over completely. With this new knowledge about myself, that I really was capable of murder, I trod the gray linoleum of the corridors. I was wearing shoes with soft soles. My footsteps were silent, the only noise being the slight swish of my white coat as I moved along. I walked with my hands in my pockets, playing with the keys nervously, for everything that had happened had given me a new receptiveness. One of the fluorescent tubes on the ceiling was flickering — it was probably a sign. That I was headed for the darkness. A door hadn't been properly closed; I noticed the small gap. On the floor, right against the molding, lay a pencil as thin and sharp as a nail. I registered this as a lack of order that wasn't normal on our ward, as if everything were about to fall apart. Anna came walking toward me, and I smiled agreeably. Once again, she put me in mind of a swan. She had the same proud carriage, the same cool purity as she sailed across the floor.

"Barbro's sleeping," she said.

I nodded. I was leaning against the wall with sagging shoulders. My posture had never been very good.

"Can you sleep at night?" she asked suddenly.

The question took me by surprise, and I gave a start.

"Not always," I confessed. "I often think about something. Something that churns and runs all night long."

She leaned against the wall as well. Relaxed her shoulders, stole a little bit of rest, lifted a hand to her blonde hair.

"What do you think about?" she asked.

"About death," I replied. "I think about death the whole time. My own death and that of others; I can't help it. People often say they're not afraid of dying. They say it in a cheerful, confident manner, seeming to be so wise and far-sighted, taking for granted that the event will be peaceful. They're going to die quietly and serenely, and in bed. They'll hardly even realize what's happening. It never occurs to them that their death might be horrible and intolerably painful—a hellish, drawn-out torture. Other people die like that, they think. I won't make a lot of fuss when it's my turn. But we do. We make a fuss. I mean, look at Barbro. I often think about such things. When I can't get to sleep."

She picked at one of her nails and glanced up at me, deadly earnest.

"And what about you?" I asked. "What's preoccupying you?"

"Is it that obvious?"

"You're not your usual sparkling self," I said.

"Well then, I must have lost some of my sparkle," she said with a mournful smile. "I think about my brother all the time. About Oscar. That he's lying at the bottom of the lake. I know it's difficult to find him, that it's dark and muddy down there. Rubbish and old tree trunks and whatnot. But I thought they gave up so quickly. And then he must have shouted," she said, "as loudly as he could. But nobody heard him. Think of it, Riktor. To be floundering in a hole in the ice and screaming at the top of your voice. And no one hears you."

In my mind's eye, I saw the red ski-suit slipping under the water.

"We don't know for certain if anyone heard him or not," I said. "Perhaps someone did hear him but couldn't do anything about it.

I mean, there are people living in the area after all. There are several houses on the shores of Lake Mester, and others on the slopes above. Maybe most of us simply shrug our shoulders if we hear someone screaming and bellowing in the distance. And just get on with what we're doing."

"What do you think went through his mind?" she asked.

I smiled gently at her.

"I imagine he thought of you. And he probably struggled as hard as he could. Don't you think he did?"

She bit her lip.

"I can't bear to think about it." She began to walk away. Then she turned suddenly, and there was anger in her low voice. "I think death is completely intolerable!"

I nodded. Certainly death was intolerable; we were in total agreement about that. I was still leaning against the wall. Anna walked away with the hem of her coat flaring like a white sail in the gray corridor.

21

RANDERS'S GREEN VOLVO came up the driveway. I could see
him from the window. I heard the engine stop and a door being
slammed. But no doorbell chimed to break the silence, so I waited.
And while I waited, my mind worked feverishly. I didn't feel
guilty, I felt betrayed. I had practically acted in self-defense. Arnfinn had dealt me a cruel blow, and my reflexes had taken over.
I could explain everything, if only someone would listen. Now
he'll go around to the back of the house, I thought suddenly, He'll
catch sight of the grave, the small mound of earth. There followed
several spine-chilling seconds while I couldn't make up my mind
what to do, although I'd been expecting him. I'd known he would
return, and I was prepared. But there was no sound of a doorbell.
Finally I went to the front door and yanked it open so abruptly
that it made him jump. He was standing on the steps with one
hand on the handrail. A broad wedding ring glinted.

"You could ring the bell," I said irately.

He gave his fleeting smile.

"You were standing at the window," he said. "You saw me coming. I didn't think it was necessary. Thanks for your assistance last
time."

He looked around the driveway.

"We need to talk. It'll take about ten minutes."

I pushed my chin forward as I do when I've been mistreated.

"You haven't asked me if it's convenient," I said sullenly.

"Is it convenient?"

"Perfectly," I said. "It's just that there are certain norms of politeness. I thought the police understood them."

He let go of the handrail and took a step nearer, leaning on the wall by the door. I felt his hot breath; it was odorless.

"Sometimes I forget about the rules," he said. "They're so time-consuming."

I led him into the hallway. Then into the living room and pointed at the corner of the sofa where he'd sat before.

"You'd better sit down."

He sat down. I took the initiative.

"Is this still about a possible murder?" I asked. "Or are you certain now?"

"I'm certain," Randers said, nodding. "And we know where to look. What to look for, who to talk to. I enjoy this phase," he said, leaning forward slightly, as was his habit. "This information-gathering phase. Finding unexpected things. Having suspicions confirmed, forming a picture of what actually happened. And last but not least, why it happened. Because there's an underlying reason for everything."

"Yes, I suppose people who kill do have something in common," I said. "Isn't that right?"

Randers considered the question. When he smiled, his eyes narrowed, and his craggy face immediately took on a milder aspect.

"Occasionally we come across unusual murderers," he declared. "Criminals who aren't like the others. With quite special motives. They never cease to astonish us."

"In what way are they unusual?" I asked. "You're a detective. Give me an example; I find this very interesting. How many pips have you got on your shoulder, by the way, when you're in uniform? I mean, are you senior to the others? You must be senior. I can see things like that right away."

Randers cocked his head.

"Three pips," he said. "But we don't bother about them much."

"Don't make me laugh."

"We're a team," Randers explained. "In which everyone has a special task. Young officers are important to us, because they're receptive to everything. People who haven't got much experience can often see things that others overlook. They aren't blinkered, so they see possibilities and unconventional solutions. Even if they do only have one pip."

"And you must be a very popular chief, Randers," I said. "A man the others look up to."

"Yes, I am," Randers asserted with self-confidence. "A very good leader, even if I say so myself. I've never been modest. Modesty isn't a virtue; it's a disability in my opinion."

I kept silent for a moment while I planned my next move.

"Where did you find the deceased?" I asked, fixing him with an unwavering expression. My heart was almost palpitating, and my cheeks were getting hot again. It was like walking on a knife-edge.

Randers paused before replying. I couldn't understand what sort of clues he'd unearthed, or what stage he'd arrived at. I couldn't believe that he was sitting in my living room, nor could I comprehend what facts had brought him to my humble red house.

"We don't need to concentrate on that," he said. "We'll deal with that later. Today I'm more interested in the incentive for taking a life."

"Motive, d'you mean?"

"Yes, certainly. Motive. Why would anyone wish to kill Nelly Friis?"

You could have heard a pin drop in my small living room. What had he just said?

Why would anyone wish to kill Nelly Friis.

I thought I'd misheard, but he really had said Nelly Friis. Nelly had been dead for a week and was shortly to be buried. And I had selected a new victim, Betzy Haugen. She was now receiving the same treatment. The thin skin behind the ear, the hair at the temple. I managed to keep my composure, but it took all the self-control I possessed. My hands lay motionless in my lap. I was dumbstruck, and it took a little while before I found my voice again.

"She's going to be buried on Friday," I managed to blurt out at last.

"She's not going anywhere until we've finished," Randers stated emphatically. "Her body has been taken to the Forensics Lab. She'll be given a postmortem."

Nelly Friis. It couldn't be true. It had to be a cruel joke; someone was poking fun at me. Randers was having a laugh at my expense, or was it merely a twist of fate? I hadn't killed Nelly. I didn't know what he was talking about. Reality seemed to be loosening its grip. Everything was topsy-turvy in my addled brain. My thoughts ran on while I searched desperately for words. For some reason, I stared up at an old ceiling rose, as if the answer to these extraordinary events might be found there.

"There's a lot you don't understand," I stammered in awkward incredulity.

"Of course," Randers replied. "And bringing the guilty party to book isn't enough for me. I need to understand."

"Some people deserve to die," I said, quickly thinking of Arnfinn. "There are people like that; I'm sure you'll agree."

He shook his head.

"I'm not getting into that. Right now we're investigating the death of Nelly Friis. Aged eighty-seven and totally dependent. Weighed about forty kilos. A thin wisp of a woman in other words. On your ward."

"But she died a natural death," I countered. "Dr. Fischer found her. She was very old and very frail, and only just clinging to life. And she was blind in the bargain."

"She didn't die naturally," said Randers. "The undertakers raised the alarm, on medical advice."

I tried to gather my wits and thought of the game of cat and mouse. It was as if fate was playing a kind of game with me, an absurd game of life and death.

"What on earth's given you the idea that it was me?" I asked. "There's a big staff there. People come visiting. Relations and friends, former neighbors and people expecting to be left something. Lots of people were in and out of that room. Didn't die naturally? People die in our care the whole time. They drop like flies. They're all on the verge of death—don't you realize that?"

I worked myself up a bit. Quite justifiably. I hadn't killed Nelly Friis. What a ludicrous idea.

"We've found some important clues," Randers said, "and they point in a definite direction." Once again, he bent forward to emphasize his own words. "And these clues indicate that we're dealing with an unusual killer. The sort we spoke of just now. The sort we never forget."

"How did she die?" I asked, struggling to stay calm.

Randers's eyes narrowed.

"I think you know the answer to that. I'm not here to supply you with details—that will come soon enough anyway. How are you feeling, Riktor?" he concluded. "Don't you feel the need to ease your conscience?"

Now it was my turn to screw up my eyes. There he was, playing his little game. Well, I could play it too.

"I haven't got a conscience," I said. "So there's nothing to ease. I do my job and I know the routines, and that's all there is to it. I don't have to feel something for every single patient. I'm not like that. But you're leveling such serious accusations that I hardly know how to treat them. To tell you the truth, I don't know what's brought you here. You're on the wrong track completely."

I gesticulated freely, my hands stressing each word.

"You'll be struggling with this case, Randers, I promise you. You'll be struggling."

"We'll see. I've got plenty of good helpers and I'm upholding the law. I have justice on my side."

"Your allegations have to be proved," I asserted. "Beyond reasonable doubt."

"In this instance, I believe we can convict you on circumstantial evidence alone," Randers said confidently. "You don't know how tenacious I am once I've made up my mind. I'm strong-willed and I like being right."

He rose and walked to the door. He turned one last time.

"Don't go anywhere. You're going to be charged. We'll be coming for you."

I stood at the window for a long while, watching his green Volvo as it drove away. And I was thoroughly dazed. No sooner had the car disappeared than I nipped out the door and ran to the back of the house. I had to check Arnfinn's grave. It still resembled a grave, but fortunately the earth had settled considerably. I decided to buy a rhododendron bush and plant it on the heap of earth. In fact, I decided to leave for the garden center right away. I went around to the driveway again and stood staring down the road. I stared until my eyes hurt but couldn't comprehend that all this had happened. One thing was very obvious. Someone was playing a game, and I'd been caught out.

I bought a fine, sturdy plant.

With a well-developed root system, strong leaves, and stems. I paid through the nose for it and carted it home on the bus, which was straightforward enough; it was wrapped in netting and rested against my legs as I sat rocking to the hum of the warm and welcoming engine. Then I got out the spade and began digging. This time it was easy because the earth had been loosened already. The rhododendron looked really nice once it was in place. Right away the small hummock appeared less noticeable, even if it did seem a bit of an odd place to plant an ornamental shrub. But I'd made up my mind. Although there weren't many callers at the house, I knew that Randers would be back. I finished off by watering the plant thoroughly with the garden hose. If only Arnfinn had known that this was all for his benefit. That even a common thief could have a beautiful bush over his final resting place. It felt good. There was a sense of finality about it. I phoned the ward and said I was ill. I couldn't face looking them in the eyes. If this were a plot, I needed time to work out a strategy. Dr. Fischer took the call. He didn't say much, and he certainly wasn't sympathetic. I'll soon be at work again, I declared, because I was quite certain of it. The things that were happening were totally absurd. I asked him to pass on my respects to Sister Anna. Remember, she's lost her brother, I exhorted. She needed support.

Dr. Fischer was abnormally reticent. Not that he'd ever been particularly forthcoming, but I noticed that he'd been affected by what had occurred. I chose to feign ignorance, but I was still feeling giddy from the strange turn my life had taken.

Then I sat down and brooded. I tried to marshal my thoughts, to form a strategy, but I was confused. That night the truck made a tremendous racket, and simultaneously I developed an almost migraine-like headache. The next day I wandered around ruminating. I stood at the window for long periods and stared out at the road, the road that I knew would bring them. I attempted to get some rest and ate some plain food. I trudged around the garden, gazed at the lovely plant on the edge of the forest, and tried to work out what was actually happening. But no matter how much I pondered, I couldn't fathom this new chain of events. Someone was making a fool of me. And from deep within, I felt a great resentment growing against the person or persons who'd caught me in a trap.

22

A TRAP.

A rotten pit into which I'd fallen headlong. The green Volvo arrived a couple of days later.

Once again, I was well prepared, because they'd announced that they were coming. But it was surreal all the same. The two men stood at the top of the steps, their legs and shoulders wide. In case I should make any attempt at resistance, but I wouldn't have even toyed with the idea. I was no fool. And besides, I was innocent, and someone who's innocent is strong. Yes, almost indecently strong — chock-full of self-assurance and right on top of the situation. I really was right on top of the situation. Randers stated his official errand firmly and concisely as his younger colleague tramped boldly past me and went into the house. He peered around everywhere, rummaging through my things. He checked the view from the windows and cast his eye over the contents of the rooms, the furniture, the desk, and the computer. He brushed his hand across shelves and tables as if searching for dust. And dust is all he found. He smiled as he caught sight of my Advent star in the window, just as Arnfinn had done. What's wrong with having a star in the window in summertime? Then he put his hands on his hips and pretended to be important. I concentrated on what Randers was saying, even though it was inexplicable. That I was suspected of aggravated murder. I held my hands out to him, palms upward, a symbolic act to show that I was innocent of the crime. It made no impression. Now at last I understood about all the suspicion at the nursing home. The evasive looks, the personal questions about how I was doing, and if I was sleeping at night; and no, I wasn't sleeping at night. I wasn't sleeping a wink. I lay tossing in torment and misery.

Then we went to the car. Randers and his young henchman sat in the front, and I sat behind them. I took nothing with me; after all, I'd soon be back, of that much I was sure. There'd never been such a miscarriage of justice as this. I mean, the murder of Nelly Friis. The car rolled down the road. The police radio crackled a bit. After a few moments, Randers broke the silence.

"What are you thinking about?" he asked, and squinted at me over his shoulder. His voice was friendly now, quite bereft of derision or triumph.

"What am I thinking about?" I gazed at the scene outside the window. "I'm thinking about the park near Lake Mester. I often go there. Have you ever been to it?"

He nodded.

"Yup, I've been there," he said. "A long time ago. Pretty little park."

"Then you must have seen the statue at the entrance to the park," I said. "Right by the paved pathway. The one that's called *Woman Weeping*."

"I have seen it," Randers replied. "Yes, it's lovely." He nodded in agreement.

"But there's another statue," I explained. "Which stands at the other end of the park. Near the exit, on the path that leads down to the lake. That one's called *Woman Laughing*. And it's her I'm thinking about now."

Randers chuckled from the front seat.

"So you think she's laughing at you?" he inquired.

"No," I countered. "She's laughing at this entire situation. Because the whole thing's so ridiculous; you can't even begin to imagine how ridiculous!"

He made no answer to this. We traveled on in silence. I stared out of the car window, at the landscape, summery greens and yellows, and the ditches gray with exhaust fumes.

"What are the remand cells like?" I asked. "Are they different from the more permanent cells?"

Randers replied over his shoulder. "A cell is a cell," he said. "You'll soon find that out."

"What about clothes? Do I wear one of those orange–colored penitentiary suits they have in America?"

"It's good you've got a sense of humor," Randers said. "You'll need it."

"I'm pretty sure old Nelly died a natural death," I said. "Dr. Fischer found her in her bed. We saw nothing unusual. So I can't understand what happened. You may not like being wrong, Randers, but this time you are. My God, how wrong you are!"

"I'm never wrong," Randers replied.

The young officer chimed in. "Randers is never wrong," he said.

"Where d'you get all this self-confidence of yours?"

"It's been acquired over many years. I know I'm cocky. Experience has made me unbearably arrogant. You'd better believe how really comfortable I am with being me," he said with a smile, "and with my job."

The whippersnapper at his side nodded. "Really comfortable!" he chorused.

"You've been allocated counsel," Randers continued. "A proper show-off. Whether you'll like him remains to be seen, but he knows his stuff. He'll give you many good bits of advice. And we in the force know most of them. But we think a few of them aren't so great. So when his professional advice is that you can refuse to say anything, don't listen to him, for God's sake. Just play ball. Otherwise the entire case will be delayed, and it'll never be over. We all benefit from your cooperation."

"What's his name, this lawyer of mine?"

"His name's de Reuter. Philip de Reuter. You two will make quite a pair."

"Will I meet him today?"

"He's already been apprised of the case," said Randers. "So he'll likely turn up. In the meantime, you can frolic in your eight square meters of cell. There's enough room in there to change your mind, regarding your guilt. And enough for a victory dance if you're found not guilty."

The court complex, police station, and county jail were housed in one gigantic building. We took the elevator from reception to the fifth floor. Then there were long linoleum-laid corridors, smelling strongly of carbolic, after which I was escorted through some double doors. Into isolation, segregation, and solitude.

Before me lay another corridor. The light there was brighter and more garish, and there was an almost cave-like silence. Narrow windows high up in the wall.

I took in the length of the corridor with only one thought in my head. That I was innocent. I hadn't killed Nelly Friis; I hadn't terminated her life in any way whatsoever. I hadn't silenced her. I'd done much, but give the devil his due. Of these things I was innocent. I was led down the corridor; I walked with a heavy tread, my body feeling feeble and apathetic, and my head teeming. On both sides were rows of green metal doors. On a couple, notes had been stuck: "CVC." Correspondence and visitor check.

"Will you put one of those on my door?"

Randers didn't answer but kept walking.

"No one will be visiting me," I said. "There'll be no one to check. And I'm guaranteed not to get any letters. So save yourselves the trouble."

I took in my surroundings and was struck by how clean it was in the prison, as if someone went around with a mop the whole time and kept the dirt at bay. The walls of the corridor were a creamy yellow. There were lots of plants and a small sofa suite with comfortable cushions. On the way, we passed a bulletin board, and I managed to glimpse the words "Holy Communion" and "Library open." A man came walking along the corridor to meet us. A sturdy-looking man with an impressive girth, like a barrel on two slender legs, and a great heavy head on a short neck. He reminded me of a fat duck. He wore a light blue shirt and had powerful hands, and keys and other equipment hung from his belt. His shoes were tough and black and very shiny. His head sprouted a shock of gray hair, which bristled in all directions.

"De Reuter will be here in an hour's time," he said. "But when he says an hour, it usually means two or three hours. He's a busy man."

We moved to one of the green doors. There was a jangling from the large bunch of keys hanging from his belt.

"To survive in here, you must learn to be patient. It's better to realize that from the word *go*. Most of your time in here is spent waiting. My name is Janson," he added. "And I'll be on duty all this week."

I entered the cramped cell and stood in the middle of it feeling bewildered, staring at the two men in the open doorway.

"What do I do if something happens?" I asked. My voice was weak, and I hated my own pathetic question. I hated them noticing my desperation, because I was proud by nature.

"Nothing much can happen in here," Janson replied, nodding at the bare, spartan room. "But we'll look after you. Just relax."

"I didn't kill Nelly Friis," I said, sinking down onto the modest bed. I held out my hands, which had begun to tremble.

"You talk to de Reuter about that," Janson said. "He's used to hearing that sort of thing."

They left and the green door slammed shut with a hard thud and the lock turned. I went straight to the window and peered out. Perhaps I was hoping that a seagull or a flock of migrating birds would fly past and lift my heart. But the misty sky was empty.

23

TOTALLY AND UTTERLY alone.

Deserted and misunderstood, my rights trampled on. Subject of a terrible mistake. Victim of a dreadful plot. Exhausted and in despair.

I'd never felt so despondent, so completely helpless. For three hours, I waited for Philip de Reuter.

In the meantime, I went over my cell inch by inch. The bed was made of gray metal. I lifted it and found that it was as heavy as lead. The wardrobe was metal, too, a cold grayish blue. There was a desk in front of the window made of a pale, unrecognizable wood, like the chair. A shelf on the wall was supported by two strong brackets. It was empty, of course. The curtains were thick and had green and blue stripes. The floor covering was gray and full of rips and blotches. There was a tiny enclosed space with a basin and toilet of brushed steel as well. It smelled of urine and lavatory cleaner. I lay down on the bed with my hands behind my head and waited for the sound of a key in the door. Waited for this de Reuter to appear and get me out. Out of this ridiculous mix-up. Preferably this very evening, because the whole thing was impossible, and I was still confused. People spent years in these cells, I mused, as I lay there trying to rest. How did they manage to survive it? Maybe they screamed all night long, thumping on the walls and banging their beds around. I wasn't sure what to expect. At the moment, it was still completely quiet. Nothing could be heard except my own nervous breathing in the room. Personally I wasn't planning any noisy demonstrations. I had a modicum of self-respect. Occasionally I dozed off, but only lightly. After a while, I began to hear a few muffled sounds. So there are people here after all, I thought; that must be Janson doing his rounds. Perhaps he'd already taken a look at me through the window in the door. The notion that someone could observe me without my knowledge was exceedingly unpleasant.

Even though I'd been expecting it, even though I'd been imagining everything that would happen from now on, I started when the key turned in the lock. I sat up. A man appeared in the door, dressed in a well-fitting suit and with a rather stylish briefcase under his arm. He was young, in his mid-thirties perhaps, with a large head of curly hair and a deep red tie like a stripe of blood from his neck. He was lean, with long, slender hands, and bright, dark eyes behind his oval glasses.

"De Reuter," he said, holding out his hand. "How are you? Have you got everything you need?"

I took his hand; it was thin and dry. He pulled the chair away from the window and moved it to the middle of the floor. He sat down, laying the briefcase on his lap. He adjusted his glasses and sent me one of those quick glances I would come to know so well. Suddenly I felt my anger rising.

"Have I got everything I need? You're not being serious, are you? I've been picked up by two policemen and hauled off to the station, and then thrown into this cramped cell. And they're claiming I've killed an old woman. And you ask if I've got everything I need? What kind of question is that?"

De Reuter didn't bat an eyelid. He sat calmly on his chair and gazed at me with his dark eyes. I noticed the creases of his trousers; they were as sharp as knives.

"We'll put a defense together," he said. "But you'll have to co-operate."

"Of course," I said, trying to calm down. "But you must get me out of this. I didn't kill Nelly Friis. We found her dead in her bed. She was eighty-seven, and I had nothing to do with it. I just want to make that clear—"

"Who was it who found her?" de Reuter cut in.

"Dr. Fischer. He'd gone in to give her an injection. He came to fetch us from the ward office to make the report. But there was nothing unusual about the death. I can't understand where these rumors have sprung from. What are they saying? The police. About how she died?"

De Reuter touched his hair with his slim, delicate hand.

"They suspect that a pillow was used," he said. "That's the way it's usually done, in murders of this type. You know, the pillow is lying there to hand, and it's all over in a minute. Randers is really on the warpath. He thinks they've got a case. It was the funeral directors who raised the alarm. Well, in consultation with Dr. Fischer. They discovered some abnormalities and contacted the police."

"What sort of abnormalities?"

"Her face seemed compressed. And there was some extravagation—leakage of blood—in her eyes. They're indications of suffocation."

He removed his glasses and looked at me intently.

"Is there anything I ought to know?"

"I've worked at Løkka for more than eleven years," I explained. "And I've never been in the habit of killing the patients. Why should I do such a thing?"

De Reuter folded his arms. Once again I was struck by his neat hands. They were like the hands of a girl, clean and white.

"At the moment, they're not saying a lot about motive. They assume that will become clear later on. As for Randers, he's the cocksure type, as I'm sure you'll have noticed. They say he can smell guilt a long way off. And without trying to be demoralizing, he does have a very high success rate. But then, so do I. So don't worry."

I rose from the bed and took a couple of short steps, but immediately ran into the desk and had to turn.

"Randers thinks he's on top of the situation," I said dejectedly. "But he's wrong. If you only knew just how wrong he is!"

"Sit down," de Reuter said calmly. "Don't fret, you'll only make yourself anxious. We'll go through everything, you and I, so that we understand each other. Do you want to plead not guilty to the charge?"

"Yes. I'm pleading not guilty," I said. "This is a conspiracy. The other staff members have turned against me, and I have no idea why. But I've noticed that something's been going on. There's been an odd feeling of ill will on the ward for a long time; that's the only way I can describe it. And I couldn't understand it. But now it's become crystal clear. They've all been plotting to get me. It's totally reprehensible."

De Reuter took out a pad and pen. He came over to the bed and put them on my lap.

"Write down the names of the people you want me to alert," he said.

"What do you mean, alert?"

"I'm thinking of friends and relatives who need to know what's happened. And where you are."

"I have no friends or relatives," I said.

"Surely you've got someone?"

"No. Nobody."

"Neighbors, perhaps?"

"I don't speak to them. No one needs to be alerted. This is a huge mistake. And if someone has killed Nelly Friis, I'll find out who did it. I work there; I know them all. There's something evil going on here. Did you hear what I said? Evil!"

De Reuter seated himself again. He seemed thoughtful.

I patted my empty trouser pockets.

"They took my keys. Will they ransack my house?"

"Will they find anything if they do?" he asked glibly.

"Of course not," I said. "A few sickly houseplants. An old computer. A bit of food in the fridge. I have no secrets in the house. When will the case come up? Will I have to spend weeks of uncertainty in here?"

"It does happen," de Reuter said. "But for your sake, I hope not. Remand is tough; it's a no man's land."

"There were plenty of other people besides me who visited Nelly Friis the day she died," I explained. "People are always dying on our ward. They're old and sick."

De Reuter shook his head. He stared down at the small blank pad.

"Not even *one* relation?"

Janson came to my cell that evening.

I liked Janson immediately, because he was strong and solid. He didn't seem concerned about what I'd been charged with but only with me and my welfare. He wanted to know if I'd got on with my lawyer. And if there was anything I needed. I had something to eat and drink and then settled on the bed. The light was beginning to fade; the sky had turned dark blue outside my cell window. There were twenty of us on the block, Janson had told me, and muffled sounds were coming from some of the other cells. It wasn't sufficient to disturb me but was more like a soothing background hum. I imagined I was a passenger in a great ship that was steaming steadily through the night.

Having lain there a good while pondering the strange state of my affairs, I finally fell asleep.

I awoke a little later in the night to hear a feeble moaning; it seemed to be coming from the adjacent cell. It was a sad, whimpering sound, and I hoped the duty officers would deal with it and calm him as quickly as possible, because the noise was increasing and getting on my nerves. It sounded as if he were begging for his life. The whining was remarkably familiar, and I listened to it with my whole being. I was also disturbed by something else. Something that gradually became all-pervasive. A ghastly smell filled the room. I thought that the smell, too, was coming from the next cell, seeping in through the ventilator I'd noticed high up on the wall. A sweet, cloying smell, the smell of something rotting.

24

MORNING CAME, AND with it the rattling of the key in the door.

Randers entered and stood there studying me, hands on hips. I saw Janson behind him take a sideways step.

"Well, we're on the move," he said, "and your defense is up and running. De Reuter doesn't hang around; you'll find that out soon enough. But neither do we. How was your night? A bit sleepless?"

I shook my head emphatically.

"I slept like a baby," I lied. "An innocent baby."

Randers crossed to the window. He stood waiting while I put my shoes on. He clasped his hands behind his back and gazed out.

"A cell with a view," he said, "that's not so bad. D'you see that large yellow building over there on the hillside? That's an old sanatorium. Some people say it's haunted. Rather a charming idea, don't you think?"

I said nothing. I was busy tying my shoelaces.

"In the evening," he continued, "when the sun goes down, all the windows glow and it looks as if the whole building's on fire. Did you notice that yesterday evening?"

I rose and walked over to him. I took in the yellow building.

"I had other things to think about yesterday evening. But I'll bear it in mind for the next sunset. Why are you here? What's happening?"

"You're going to be questioned," he said. "Come on, let's go."

We descended through the building to a bare, cellar-like room, with two chairs and a table and nothing else in its windowless interior. It could have been a mountain cave. The walls were rough and gray and the light was unpleasant, but once we were seated, he switched off the strip lights in the ceiling and turned on a small desk lamp.

"I think I've got the right to have my lawyer present," I protested.

Randers sent me a broad, agreeable grin.

"Why yes, you have," he conceded. "But de Reuter is busy elsewhere, so there's just you and me. Let's try to get a bit of momentum into this case; that will reduce the length of remand. And that's what you want, isn't it? To get it all over quickly? Shall we begin?"

I made no reply. I tried to understand the extraordinary situation I found myself in, and attempted to rise above it, but it didn't work. Randers seemed so certain, and that made me deeply nervous. I'd never met a man with so much self-confidence. He knew something — something I'd overlooked — but I couldn't fathom what it was. I felt a little off balance and continually perplexed. Randers now had control over everything. Over the questions he would ask and the time it would take until I was again led back to my austere cell.

"You chose to work with old people," he began. "You chose to use your nurse's training on the most sick and helpless patients. Tell me why that was."

I folded my hands on the table while a heaviness spread through my whole body. I thought about Arnfinn constantly, and whether they'd find him beneath the rhododendron bush I'd planted on the small mound of earth, if they went to the house. And how I'd explain what had happened.

"I have a special way with the elderly," I said. "Not just the elderly, but people who are close to death. Those are the patients we take. I understand their requirements and their care needs. And I like the work at Løkka. It's a quiet, peaceful place, most of the time at least. Not like the bustle of an accident and emergency department or a large hospital."

"A special way," Randers said, scratching his chin. "I see. You know what they need? Well, it's really wonderful you've got these talents. So, if I sent my old mom in, she'd be in safe hands with you?"

He looked directly at me.

"In the very best of hands," I said, and returned his gaze.

"And this talent for caring, how do you deploy it?"

I had to think. I had to weigh my mendacious words. "I like making a difference to people's lives," I explained. "I like to feel significant because I believe I am."

"You're often in their rooms," said Randers. "Your colleagues mentioned that. Are you the type of nurse who likes sitting by patients' bedsides? I mean, the sort we have so few of?"

He adjusted the lamp on the table a little. The light fell on my face, and I felt the heat from it.

"Yes, I do like that."

"But have you got time? People who work with the elderly are always complaining that they don't have enough time. I'm only asking because of what I've read. According to the newspapers, you're almost too rushed to get your patients out of bed in the mornings."

"I don't hang around the ward office, like a lot of the others," I said. "My job would be meaningless if I weren't able to give them that bit of extra care. I'd have thrown in the towel and done something completely different. And anyway, hardly any of them even leave their beds. They're too ill for that."

Randers took notes. Biting the top of his pen, he glanced up at me with narrowed eyes.

"You've never started a family, Riktor. Was it a conscious decision?"

"It's just the way things have turned out," I explained. "Relationships and family life aren't easy for me. It must be a talent I haven't got."

I stared down at the floor. He was getting close to my sore spot, that I'd never had a woman. Never in all my miserable life had I had a woman.

"But what about children, Riktor? Someone as caring as you. Don't you miss children?"

"I don't want children," I said. "Not at any price. I mean, you can never escape them once they're born; it's an endless responsibility. And I like being in control. There's a lot wrong with living alone," I added, "but I can at least do what I want with my days and nights. I'm in charge of all the plans and decisions. I can go out when I like, and there's no one expecting me back."

"In other words, no one places any demands on you."

"Correct," I said. "It's called freedom."

"Or loneliness," he said. "But, OK. I can understand that. Would you say that you had a special relationship with Nelly Friis?"

I thought for some time, mulling the matter over a little.

"I've got a special relationship with every one of my patients. And I regard them as adults and individuals deserving dignity. If I'd considered a mercy killing, I wouldn't have chosen Nelly Friis. I'd have chosen Barbro Zanussi. Barbro lives in a torment of pain. She lies groaning all day long, and it's a strain on everybody."

"So the person who killed Nelly did it out of kindness. Is that what you think?"

I nodded. "And so do you. Such angels of death do occasionally turn up in old people's homes and institutions. I've read about them in the papers—strange, distracted characters who are drawn to such work. But we only have one angel on our ward. That's Sister Anna Otterlei, and she's completely flawless."

"What's your attitude toward death, Riktor? Can you tell me a bit about that?"

"I'm painfully aware of it," I said, "and I see it happening to others. But I keep hoping it won't happen to me."

Randers chuckled and wrote. I sat thinking about our conversation and then wondered if my house was being turned upside down. There were some muffled thumping noises coming from the corridor, a voice and a door slamming.

"So how did Nelly Friis die?" I asked after a long silence.

Randers lowered his pen. He sat looking at me for a time and then clasped his hands on the table.

"The postmortem showed that she'd been suffocated. She had blood leakage in her eyes. There were tooth marks on the inner surface of her upper lip, something that occurs when a lot of pressure is applied to the mouth. Her nose had been pressed down hard. Considerable force was used."

"Nobody said anything about that at the time," I objected. "Dr. Fischer pronounced her dead. There were no suspicions of that sort, no discussion. I don't understand how this has arisen in the first place. If I was the suspect, why didn't they say that immediately?"

"You need time to build up a case," Randers said. "And now at last we've got a case. How are you feeling?" he asked all of a sudden. "Obviously it's quite a strain being questioned, with such a grave charge hanging over one's head."

"It's no strain on me," I said staunchly. "Because I didn't kill Nelly Friis. I'm completely innocent."

Randers was calm and collected. He was buoyant and self-assured, one of those thoroughly successful types. And I really did wonder what evidence he had. Surely they couldn't condemn me on mere assumptions?

Although I was reasonably articulate and did quite well in this first interview, it was a relief to be escorted back to my cell. Janson locked the door behind me, and I immediately sat down at the window. I laid my arm on the desk in front of me and looked at my own hand and the way it was slightly flexed. It was as if time were standing still. All sounds from the block seemed far away, and I tried to relax. But my thoughts kept racing the whole time, like a mill churning incessantly, around and around.

What was really happening?

After a while, I stretched out on the bed, with my hands cradling my head. I tried to breathe calmly. I imagined the park by Lake Mester, which I missed so sorely—its splashing water, its green benches. *Woman Weeping* and *Woman Laughing*. Ebba's crocheting needle flashing in the sunlight. I thought about Anna's brother, who was still at the bottom of the lake. Perhaps the eels had gnawed deep holes in the dissolving flesh. And eaten his eyes. Occasionally I dozed. But all the time a part of me was waiting for Janson's key.

25

DE REUTER APPEARED the next afternoon, this time in a dark blue suit and stylish turquoise tie, perfectly knotted. He sat down at the desk. He wanted to know if I was abreast of things and understood what was happening.

"I simply want justice," I said, "like everyone else. I don't mind being judged for the small things I've done, but not for this. I really do find it hard to grasp that this is even happening. Why have they all turned against me? I thought they were decent colleagues. Not to put too fine a point on it: I feel thoroughly betrayed."

De Reuter unzipped his briefcase with verve. Papers rustled.

"There's just one thing I've got to get straight, if you don't mind," he said, his dark eyes resting on me.

"Yes?" I asked doubtfully.

"You mustn't conceal things from me."

"What are you talking about?"

"What I mean," he explained, "is this. I don't want any unpleasant surprises sprung on me when I'm in court. There must be no secrets. We must be open with each other."

"You won't have any unpleasant surprises," I assured him. "These are simply groundless accusations. And when the day of the trial comes, I'll have my answers ready; I can promise you that."

"Did you see Nelly after she was dead?"

"She was carried down to the basement, and her next of kin could go and see her. Yes, I did make a quick visit to the mortuary to say goodbye. It's always a little sad; she'd been with us a long time. She was like a sparrow. Tiny and thin and blind."

De Reuter sat watching me as I spoke. I couldn't imagine him with a family and a wife, with brats running around clinging to his legs. I couldn't imagine him working in the garage or watching saucepans, or even having a life beyond this. He's probably always a lawyer, I thought. Always on his way to some cell or other, with an overfilled office for a base, where his volumes of Norwegian Statutes shine red and ponderous on the shelves. And if he had a woman, she'd be a lawyer too. Perhaps they shared an office. Perhaps they sat opposite each other as they worked, their glances meeting once in a while across the piles of papers.

"When we're in court, it's important that you show respect," he pointed out. "And preferably, a considerable degree of humility too. It creates a good impression; it's what they want to see. The jury can't be bought, but they're not impossible to charm and persuade. Remember all this when we're in court."

"It's not easy to show humility when you're innocent," I protested. "Because I'm pretty furious really, and I have a right to be."

"Then you must check yourself," de Reuter returned. "And remember this. The court is looking for civility."

He took me through my entire life, more or less. My childhood and adolescence, of which I could tell him little apart from small confusing fragments. He particularly wanted to know about my relationship with my parents and with others of my own age.

"I had no relationships whatsoever," I explained. "Not with anyone."

"But, what about your mother?"

"Well, she brought me up well. I'm very independent. I don't rely on others; I don't think one should."

"And Nelly Friis? What was your relationship with her?"

"I suppose I was rather fascinated," I said. "Nelly was blind, and I'd thought a lot about what it would be like to live in darkness. The thing is, I don't experience the dark in the same way as other people do."

De Reuter turned his eyes to me.

"So tell me how you experience the dark," he said.

"I can see anyway. Every object seems to have remnants of light left in it, which enables me to see the outline of everything, even when it's pitch-black. I can also make out surfaces and spaces. They pulsate with an orange-colored light. I've always had this ability, but I've never found any explanation for it. I've probably got more receptors than other people. Let me put it this way: I've always felt myself to be somewhat different and unusual."

De Reuter made a short note. A tiny crease of anxiety appeared between his eyes.

"Don't mention that in court," he said.

"No?"

"People may take it the wrong way."

"What do you mean?"

"They may think you're a bit mad. And we must avoid that. So, you can see in the dark, can you? Well, I never. I'll go and make a fair copy of these notes now and get to work. I'll visit as often as I can. Let me know if there's anything you need; don't be afraid to ask. I've got quite a number of clients, but your case is an interesting one, so I'll be following it closely. Apart from that, are they treating you with respect?"

I gave him a sour smile and wondered if he was naive or if it was simply that he was living in a completely different world.

After he left, I stood and looked around my cell. I realized I could choose one of three ways to pass the time. I could lie on my bed with my hands behind my head. I could pace the small floor with calm, deliberate steps to keep my circulation going. Or I could sit at the desk in front of the window and watch the sun's reflected glow in the panes of the sanatorium.

26

I WAS REMANDED in custody by the court for four weeks. When the time was up, it was extended by another four weeks. De Reuter had prepared me, and I didn't let myself get worn down. I was ready to fight. I had a series of interviews with Randers in which I repeatedly declared my innocence and constantly reassured him of my first-class qualities as a caregiver. But he continued to remain cocksure that I'd committed the murder. This worried me because I couldn't understand what it was based on. I clung to de Reuter, which was distasteful to me, since he who stands alone is strongest—well, that's my theory. But he was my only hope in this difficult situation. And I felt he believed in my innocence, even though he claimed that it wasn't exactly that he was interested in. He was simply working on damage limitation, as he put it. Nelly Friis was dead. Someone had to pay, but not more than necessary; that was his thinking. He had little time for revenge. And, in his view, that was the sole concern of our legal system.

Society took revenge on behalf of the injured party. As if that could achieve anything, apart from ruining another human life.

It would be wrong to say that I and my lawyer became close. I'd heard of that sort of thing happening, but it didn't happen in our case. I was fairly standoffish. But I was quite talkative during my interviews with Randers. Time and again I tried to explain that the others had gone behind my back. No one had breathed a word that there was anything unusual about Nelly's death. She was collected by the undertaker and driven away, and we got on with our work. A new patient was being admitted because we had an empty bed. Randers often wanted to talk about my previous job at another nursing home, where I'd been employed for more than six years. There, too, they'd ganged up against me in a most unpleasant way. Until finally I'd decided to leave of my own free will. I had never been the argumentative type. I got on well with Janson. I never caused trouble in my cell, and I followed all the rules to the letter. As de Reuter had recommended.

Don't be a difficult prisoner.

It never pays in the long run.

I'd habituated myself to the small space, the view from the window, and the hard bed. The prison food was excellent. So good that I had to ask Janson who worked in the kitchen.

"Margareth makes the food," he told me. "And she has an assistant to help her. Oh yes, she's a dab hand at the cooking. We're glad she's here, because we pinch a bit of grub ourselves, the staff here do; I won't deny it. You mustn't let on if there's an inspection because it's against the rules. How're things apart from that? Are you managing to get through the nights OK?"

I mentioned the moaning from the adjoining cell, but he only gave me a blank look.

"No moaning persons in here," he said. "You must've dreamed it."

I mentioned the ventilator on the wall just below the ceiling and that at times a foul smell had seeped into the cell while I was sleeping. He glanced up at the wall and then shook his great head.

"The only thing that comes in through that ventilator is fresh air," he maintained, and stared sympathetically at me because that was the sort of man he was.

"I'll tell you something," he said. "Many of the people who've been here a long time have problems when they finally leave. The world is too large, things happen too quickly, the noise is unbearable, the crowds in the streets are overwhelming. One of our charges finally got prison leave after serving four years. He hadn't been in town half an hour before he collapsed."

27

ONCE AGAIN MY life took a new and unexpected turn.

Janson, who worked tirelessly for the inmates, had managed to convince the other staff that I should be allowed to work in the kitchen. With Margareth. For a few hours each day. Because I had no family or friends who came to visit me and no relatives who wrote or phoned.

I had no one.

Other inmates occupied themselves in the workshop, making bookshelves and furniture. Others again used the gym or studied in the library, trying to better themselves. But I was going to get kitchen work. I imagined that this Margareth must be rather a special person, as she'd chosen to cook for murderers and bank robbers.

Margareth was about the same age as me. She wasn't much to look at, at least not at first glance. Perhaps I was being unkind, but I knew beauty when I saw it—and sadly, she was no beauty. She had dry, carrot-colored hair and pointed elf-like ears. Dr. Scholl's on her feet, a faded apron with pockets, and an old-fashioned mauve blouse. The mauve made her own color seem pale and slightly bluish. She came forward to meet me, her arms folded over her stomach, tight-lipped and with a sharp, appraising eye.

"Can you use a knife?" she asked.

"I'm charged with murder," I said and smiled, trying to be funny. "But I'm innocent," I added. "Just so you know."

"That's what they all say," was Margareth's response. "Nobody in here is guilty of anything. I'm not guilty, either," she went on, "but I have to come here and work myself to the bone just the same. That's what things have come to."

She weighed me up from top to toe, as if to see what sort of stuff I was made of. Then she turned and went to the work surface and began tidying. One of her stockings had a run in it. I said nothing. One didn't insult a woman in that way.

"Well," she said, "we might as well make a start. We're preparing lunch. You can chop fruit and vegetables for the salads. Wash your hands over there, and do it properly. I'm keeping an eye on you. We don't want any food poisoning here, because when twenty people are ill all at the same time, it's a nightmare. And I'm speaking from bitter experience."

I nodded like some mechanical puppet, clenched my teeth, and did as I'd been told. Margareth got out a chopping board and two knives, a small one with a short, pointed blade and another slightly larger one with a serrated edge. She went to the fridge and took out fruit and greens: sweet peppers, mushrooms, and cucumber, lettuce, beetroot, apples, oranges, and grapes. She placed them on my work surface and nodded. Her movements were swift and efficient; she was obviously used to working quickly.

I found myself in an oasis. Of course, there was a lot of steel and plastic, and the ceramic tiles glinted coldly, but after endless weeks alone in that bare cell, the fruit and vegetables crowding my work surface were like a fresh and luxuriant world.

"Peppers into thin rings," Margareth explained, "and the cucumber sliced. Just dice the mushrooms. There's an apron over there on the wall you can wear. I'll get some salad bowls for you to put it all in. Then we'll make a dressing of oil and vinegar. We wheel the food out to the common room on trolleys. Off you go now. Lunch has to be ready by midday."

I was keen to make a good impression on Margareth. There was no one else in my life, besides the prison officers who came and went. De Reuter with his astute glances, and Randers who had brought me down for questioning. After giving my hands a long, thorough wash, I rinsed away the soap and dried them with a paper towel from a dispenser on the wall. I tied on the apron and rolled up my sleeves, selected the serrated knife, and held it for an instant in my hand. I felt hugely contented with this new facet of prison life, which had so unexpectedly come my way. I studied Margareth out of the corner of my eye. She bustled back and forth in her apron like a busy bee. Her hair really was quite a sight, a carrot-colored wave, almost like a flame on the top of her head. Her cheeks were pale and thin and adorned with large freckles. Her eyelashes, carefully darkened with mascara, were surprisingly long.

"Thinner rings," she commanded, as I stood working on a pepper. "You'll have to peel the cucumber. Leaving the skin on makes it taste of grass. Just in case you didn't know."

"I do know," I replied.

I felt myself breaking into a smile once more. I almost wanted to begin waltzing around the floor, but I set my jaw and concentrated on looking earnest and industrious. I chopped in deep concentration. My knife was sharp and made easy work of the fruit and vegetables, and I applied myself to it, hungry as I was for variety and appreciation. Margareth stood next to me, slicing bread with a machine. After that she made butter balls and formed them into a neat pyramid, over which she sprinkled parsley. It resembled a Christmas tree. I noticed that her hands were large and rough and there was no ring on her finger. But that didn't mean she didn't have anyone, although somehow I rather doubted it. She seemed a bit stubborn and unapproachable, not a person who wins over others. But I felt an immediate bond of intimacy with her. It came completely unbidden, as if nature had placed us on the same wavelength—both of us behind these walls for an unspecified period. We made two large bowls of salad. I sprinkled dressing over the vegetables and squeezed orange juice over the fruit.

"Now," said Margareth, "we'll put it all on the trolleys. We need some cheese and meat to go on open sandwiches. Can you use an electric carver?"

I nodded. I fetched ham and salami from the fridge and felt a kind of childish joy because I was standing here next to Margareth in the kitchen. I forgot almost everything else—forgot where I was and why, forgot that my life had fallen apart and that my future was uncertain.

"Do you know Randers?" I asked, after a few moments' silence.

Margareth nodded.

"Everyone knows Randers," she said.

She chewed her thumbnail and nodded once more.

"He comes in here from time to time pinching food. At first I found him pretty unbearable, but now I've gotten used to him. I suppose we've just got to accept that some people live on the sunny side. That they're lucky and successful in life. But that's not how my life has been, God knows. Ah, well," she concluded, and placed the dish of butter balls on the trolley. Never in all my life had I seen such a perfect pyramid of butter balls.

"Do the men like that?" I asked, indicating the dish.

"Oh, they're like little kids. They're so disappointed if the pyramid's not quite up to standard. Once you've started, you can't get out of it, because they're so used to it. And then, I like a bit of fun myself."

"I haven't seen any women on the block," I said. "Aren't there any female prison officers here?"

For a few moments, Margareth was silent. Her bony hands ceased in their activity and rested on the work surface, and her eyes under their darkened lashes became distant.

"No, no women," she said at length. "Apart from me, that is, but I suppose I don't count."

"So have there never been any?"

Margareth lifted a hand to her eye, perhaps to wipe a tear, I thought.

"A long time ago, there was a girl working here," she said. "Well, I say a girl because she was only twenty-something. Her name was Linda, and everyone liked her a lot. She worked hard on behalf of the inmates and their rights. And she was fearless too," she added. "Positive and caring. She was a good-looking girl, make no mistake. Many a yearning glance followed her when she patrolled the corridors, I can tell you."

She picked up a raisin and popped it in her mouth. Chewed it for a while.

"She wore her long blonde hair in a ponytail. I once told her she ought to get rid of it, that sooner or later one of the men here would grab it and pull her down. If you know what I mean. Well, sometimes they snap, and they grab whatever's at hand. Spectacles. And ears, and that kind of thing. I expect you can imagine. But she wouldn't listen, and she kept her long blonde hair."

Margareth said nothing for a while, and then she looked straight at me.

"They went to the cinema one evening—she went with one of the prisoners here. His name was Frank and he was in for murder, sentenced to sixteen years. Frank was very strong. And had a brain the size of a pea, if the truth be told. He spent practically the whole day working out in the gym, and he got bigger with every month that passed. Then he was granted an evening's leave and permission to go to the cinema. And Linda was to accompany him. Can you believe the management consenting to something like that?"

I didn't answer. Margareth continued.

"They went off early that evening in a van, and they never returned."

"Did they abscond?" I asked stupidly.

"He killed her," Margareth said. "After the film. The van was parked in a copse, and they found her lying in the grass next to it. Most of her blonde hair had been ripped off. Frank was caught a couple of days later and immediately admitted the crime. But he never gave a motive for it. Presumably he'd made advances to her, and she'd refused, naturally. She could hardly have done otherwise. Lads with big muscles don't like getting no for an answer. What on earth's wrong with them? Everyone gets rejected now and then. I've been rebuffed more times than I care to remember. That's life. Not everyone wants us, after all."

That rings a bell, I thought to myself, and gave Margareth a sideways glance. If only I had a woman.

She took another raisin.

"So you see," she continued, "after that affair, our managers have never dared to employ women again. That would have brought it all back again. And we couldn't bear to be reminded of that. Yes, it was awful what happened to Linda. Truly awful."

Margareth finished speaking and carried on with her work. She bustled around adding the final touches, mixing juice in two large jugs and placing the beetroot in small bowls. I cast my eye over it all, and I thought that never before had colors seemed so bright and vivid and radiant. The beetroot was as wet and dark as blood, and it dyed her lips red when she put a slice in her mouth.

"Is Frank still on the block?" I inquired.

"No, he's in Oslo Prison. So you won't be bumping into him

around here. The other inmates turned against him, so he had to be transferred."

"What about your assistant?" I asked. "What's happened to him?"

"He's on long-term sick leave," Margareth answered. "It seems to be a problem with his bones; he's got pains all over his body. That's the only reason you've been given this opportunity," she added. "Not because you're special or unusual in any way, but because it means they don't need to employ a stand-in and that saves them money. And if you work well, they'll let you stay in the kitchen for a good while."

28

MARGARETH.

I hadn't registered her surname, only Margareth. I went around savoring the name, moving it around my mouth, rolling it across my tongue, letting it fill my head and heart. Margareth. The name was like a little tune; the name was pleasant and warm, and perhaps just a tiny bit lonely. Margareth, Margareth. With beetroot juice on her lips, and her light blue eyes fringed with black lashes. I imagined a simple juxtaposition. Margareth and Riktor. Didn't that sound like a couple, like two souls that belonged together? There was something about the chime and rhythm of the names. They went so perfectly together: Margareth and Riktor. Suddenly I fancied that there was a more profound meaning to my life so far. Everything I'd undergone, the many interrogations and the forlorn cell, the false accusations. The betrayal. All the time I'd been journeying toward Margareth. I was certain this was right and that the future held something. Something I needed and wanted, had always wanted. As if in a vision I saw it: an entirely new perspective. Margareth and I in the park near Lake Mester, together on a green bench. I paced around my cell thinking of these things, thinking of Eddie and Janne, and the joy of being a couple.

At length I sank down on the chair. The sanatorium on the opposite hillside, which I could see through the bars, had four rows of windows, and there were twenty windows in each story; I'd counted them. It was no longer used as a sanatorium, but was now a rehabilitation center for heart patients. I thought of all the people lying in their beds behind the windows, with hearts that suddenly, and possibly without warning, had stopped beating. Or beat irregularly, or much too fast, and I thought of their fear of dying. I imagined them lying in their beds with hands on their chests, checking. Those continuous contractions that were so vital to us. There was nothing wrong with my own heart; it beat steadily all day long with energetic persistence. What was it Arnfinn had said about his heart? It beat like an Opel engine. But during those interviews with Randers, my pulse did occasionally rise.

De Reuter worked tirelessly.

He often popped into my cell, or we would sit in a visiting room, but he realized I was managing fine and would soon leave again. Janson took me into the exercise yard so that I could feel the sun on my face. I sensed it was warming me in a new and promising way now after my meeting with Margareth; I could almost feel the vitamins penetrating my skin. Janson would sit on a bench and smoke a cigarette, while I made slow circuits of the yard.

"How old is Margareth?" I inquired, halting in front of him.

"Well," said Janson, taking his time. "She must be getting on for fifty, wouldn't you think? Or maybe forty-five? She's from the north," he said, "and she's a widow. Her husband was killed on the railway, many years ago now. Nasty business. Some shock that must've been."

"Killed on the railway?" I said in horror. I put my hands on my hips and looked aghast at Janson. "How? Was he in a car? Or walking along the line?"

"It's all a bit vague," Janson said, flicking the ash off his cigarette. "Don't try asking questions about it, or she'll chuck you out of the kitchen. She won't ever speak about what happened."

I went on walking in wide circles. I stuck my fingers through the wire fence that surrounded us, and smelled the scent of grass from the other side, the tang of the freedom that had been taken from me. It never occurred to me that I might be found guilty of Nelly's murder because I had some belief in justice. But the other thing, the thing that had happened to Arnfinn, was quite a different matter. I could defend myself there, too, if it came to it. I peered up at the prison wall with its rows of windows, each covered by a grate of rusty metal. The surrounding area was dominated by the building, old and gray and ponderous, and the netting fence was topped with great rolls of barbed wire. They were like huge birds' nests. But I knew that people had escaped. I had no such plans myself, and I was eagerly anticipating the start of my case. Then I would rise to my feet in court, stand tall, and tell the truth.

Again I stopped in front of Janson.

He was smoking his roll-up and squinting at the sun.

"I don't suppose innocent people are often found guilty, are they?" I asked.

"No," Janson said, "but it does happen. And the guilty are sometimes acquitted." He drew on his cigarette, exhaling the smoke in big white clouds. "Either way, it's equally bad in my opinion. But the system isn't foolproof, and the law is the law. But Randers is notorious for getting at the truth," he went on, nodding toward the wing of the building where the inspector had his office.

I had to face the fact: I might have to serve years for a murder I hadn't committed. While the other crime, against Arnfinn, remained undiscovered. The notion took my breath away, and

I couldn't whisper a word about it to a living soul. I carried it with me in the same way as the secret about the skier who went through the ice. I couldn't mention him either; people wouldn't understand. I seated myself on the bench next to Janson. He exuded a friendly calm. As if life's difficulties had never touched or troubled him. I enjoyed sitting there in the sun, with the cigarette smoke drifting slowly past.

"You never get any visitors," he commented tentatively.

"No, that's right. And I'm not worried about it, either. I haven't got that much to say to other people. Apart from Margareth, that is."

"There's a system of prison visitors," Janson continued. "If you want, you can add your name to the list. Then you'll have a visit every fortnight, or just once a month, if you prefer. That is, if we find someone."

"Prison visitors?" I said, wrinkling my nose. "Who would want to do that?"

Janson trod out his cigarette. He retrieved the butt and put it in his tobacco pouch, which he slipped into his inside pocket.

"Socially minded people. Often well into middle age. Or sometimes retired folks who've got a bit of time on their hands; they frequently volunteer for it. But there are younger people, too; those who're interested and prepared to give the time. The Red Cross organizes the service for inmates who want it. So, what do you think, Riktor?"

I thought it over for a while.

"What if I get someone I can't stand?" I objected.

"Try to be a bit positive," Janson exhorted and gave me a slap on the shoulder. "Think about it."

I stood up and began walking again. After a few circuits, I stopped by the fence and gazed over at him.

"At least Nelly lived to be old," I said. "And she died in her own bed. Because of some motive or other, I don't know what. She also had a respectable funeral. Think of all those people who are never found. Who die in the forest without anybody knowing about it, or drown and end up at the bottom of a lake."

"It's depressing all right," Janson replied. "It's important to have a grave. D'you think about things like that a lot?" He stood and felt his pocket. "Well, let's be having you, then. Time's up."

I was innocent.

I lay on my bed and sat by the window. I mooched around my cell, taking short paces to and fro across the frayed, gray flooring. I splashed cold water in my face and contemplated revenge. Revenge germinated down at my feet and then rose, working its way through my system. Sometimes I found it hard to breathe because it had thoroughly got the better of me. I planned to make someone pay for the misfortune that'd hit me so hard. The real culprit was sitting somewhere rubbing his hands. It was unbearable. I counted the hours and days and weeks, and de Reuter kept me informed of the case's progress. Every time he arrived, he was wearing a colorful tie. Mustard yellow with his dark suit, red or blue ties with the gray. Randers kept fetching me for more questioning. He was never going to give in, and I was pretty worn out. I spoke the truth for several hours and my lies were only white ones. I was filled with righteous indignation. In my mind's eye, I saw my own magnificent performance in court. And de Reuter explained the layout of the courtroom.

"The witnesses will give their evidence on your left," he said, "and the public prosecutor will be on your right. The judge and the jury will be directly opposite you, so you can look them in the eye. Do that—look them right in the eye. The courtroom is large and oval with blue, high-backed chairs. Windows right up to the ceiling. There are carafes of water as well as pens and paper and microphones so that people can hear. You must get there prepared, rested, and well dressed. Don't interrupt anybody and don't get worked up. Make sure to keep your temper under control; that's important. If something unexpected happens, it's essential to keep calm. I'll be with you all the way. Also, it's possible I may correct you during the proceedings, if I think you're breaking any of our rules or agreements. If I'm to get you off, I must be in complete control."

29

MARGARETH RECEIVED ME in her large tiled kitchen every day. With its brushed-steel gadgets and gleaming work surfaces. At first she was fairly taciturn, but her tongue gradually loosened. She told me about her early years in northern Norway and how tough it had been, with little money and a hard, rugged climate. The endless, freezing winter months when it was dark almost all day long. She never raised her eyes as she spoke, and she hardly ever looked into mine. Either she was very shy by nature or simply unwilling to look at me—I was never quite sure. Her attention was always on her work. A piece of meat or a raw fish, whatever she might be working on. I'd never seen hands so swift: they skinned, filleted, and jointed with lightning speed.

Margareth, I mused, as I trotted at her heels like a puppy. Here come Margareth and Riktor. Every Friday we worked out a menu for the coming week. I loved these interludes, sitting close together at the table, pen and paper at the ready.

"Monday," Margareth kicked off. "Start of another week. And hardly the best day for any of us, I shouldn't think. The weekend's so far away. Well, what do you think, Riktor?"

She spoke my name. She spoke it loud and clear. It sounded so fine when she said it, as if I were hearing it for the first time. She rubbed the corner of her eye with a knuckle, and a bit of mascara streaked her cheekbone.

"Something hot," I recommended. "Something to set the palate on fire, something Mexican—tacos, for example, or chili con carne."

"With bread and butter and salad," Margareth said as she nodded. "Yes, I think that'll be good. We'll go for chili."

She noted it on her menu sheet. Her handwriting was messy; I could only read it because I knew what she'd written. Her bleached apron still had traces of beetroot juice that hadn't come out in the wash, and she was wearing the mauve blouse that couldn't have suited her less.

"We'll need a cool pudding," she volunteered. "What d'you think, Riktor? Ice cream?"

I proposed yogurt with fresh berries.

"I can see you're not in charge of the budget," Margareth mumbled. "Well, we'll just have to economize later in the week."

"We could have pancakes on Tuesday," I said. "They're easy and cheap. Pancakes with bacon and maple syrup. Then we'll have to serve up fish on Wednesday; I know you'll agree with that."

And so we sat working at the table. I dictated and Margareth wrote. We'd become a team. The thought that her kitchen assistant would one day return and push me out was unbearable. I didn't want to lose what I'd found at long last, these moments with Margareth. Surely fate couldn't be so unkind, I reasoned; wasn't it my turn to have a bit of luck now, after all that had happened?

Janson often popped in. He wanted to check that I was behaving well. And where Margareth was concerned, everything I did was impeccable.

. . .

Then a most unexpected thing happened.

I actually had to put out a hand, searching almost for something to steady me, as I tried to comprehend a quirk of fate so astonishing that it left me speechless and only able to stand there dumb and irresolute. Janson had escorted me to a visiting room. For a meeting with a woman called Neumann. "A woman of a certain age," Janson had said. "She's been an accountant all her life, and a prison visitor for many years at various institutions. She's got lots of experience. She'll be here at two."

Now she was standing there, in the open doorway.

With red lips and a stiff perm. Ebba from the park near Lake Mester. *She* was my prison visitor. Her eyes opened in amazement as she saw me, and then she controlled herself as much as she could to smooth over her own huge surprise at finding me, Riktor, waiting for her. Riktor the prisoner. Charged with murder.

But I soon recovered and, as we'd suddenly been thrown together like two dice in a box, made the best of a bad situation. We shook hands. She had a firm grip. She wasn't embarrassed for an instant; instead I noticed a humorous smile spread over her red mouth. She regained her composure and unbuttoned her jacket; her movements were assured, calm, and well rehearsed. There was a secureness deep within her person, which had a comforting effect. I sat down.

"Well, this is a surprise," she admitted. "But I'm the type that gets over surprises quickly." She pulled out the other chair, straightened her clothes, and patted her hair, taking her time. "We've met before, of course. And I did sometimes wonder what had become of you because you used to come to the park so frequently. But now I know why."

She settled herself on the chair. Knees pressed together, a hand up to her hair.

"Life isn't kind to everyone, that's for sure," said Ebba Neumann. Despite the shock, her voice was firm and steady. She was doubtless a woman who was used to speaking at meetings, a woman who'd rise when the situation demanded it and say a few wise and unifying words.

She put her handbag on the floor. A brown handbag of imitation crocodile skin, with a large gold-colored clasp. She sat with her body and head erect, the neat undulations of her gray hair receding in waves from her brow.

"What have they told you?" I asked. "About why I'm here; have they said anything?"

Her hands rested serenely in her lap, like thin, curled insects. One of her fingers had two plain gold rings on it, her own and her husband's, I thought; presumably he was dead. Her nails were varnished and looked like mother-of-pearl.

"Not a thing," said Ebba. "And it's none of my business. You haven't been found guilty of anything. As I understand it, you're on remand. And to put your mind at rest, I know how to keep my mouth shut. Please forgive my presumption, but in spite of everything, you're looking well."

She took off her jacket and hung it over the back of the chair. She had long, shapely legs and wore gossamer-thin stockings; I could make out finely branching veins through the delicate mesh.

"If you knew what I was accused of, you'd be shocked," I said.

Suddenly I was overcome with bitterness over all that had happened. That I was being held in this institution for an indefinite period, totally without grounds, totally without guilt. So friendless and alone that the Red Cross had to send an old woman to keep me company. I'd been insulted and humiliated, but I was glad she was sitting there. She was a link to the park, to the time before all this happened, to the good and disciplined life that I'd had control over.

"Possibly so," she conceded, "but we don't have to talk about that. Just for the record, though, I do read the newspapers. And there's been a lot of comment about what happened."

Naturally the press had reveled in it. The nurse from Løkka, and all the things he'd been up to. The lunatic care worker. These lies. This conspiracy, this whole rotten thing.

"Then you know everything there is to know," I said. "That's the way of the world now, we're informed about almost everything that happens. And you become my prison visitor. I don't know how you dare."

"Shouldn't I dare?"

I gave her a long, hard appraisal. Her hair, her hands with their rings, her feet in their brown court shoes with small bows. This eminently elegant woman I'd seen so many times before. Who might even be on my side, in spite of everything.

"There comes a day when we get out of prison," I said to Ebba. "And then we might come after you. Follow you, beg. Call up, and be a nuisance, and annoy you. People turn into stray dogs when they're released; that's what the prison officers say. Haven't you ever considered that?"

Ebba gave a long and hearty laugh. It was the first time I'd heard her laughter: it was deep, infectious, and redeeming. Automatically I thought of *Woman Laughing*; it was the same warm sound that came to my inner ear when I passed that evocative sculpture at the park entrance.

"No," she said, smiling. "I'm not frightened that you'll come after me. Or follow me. Or beg for anything. I'm not scared of dogs, either."

"You've probably been warned to keep quiet about yourself. About where you live, what you do, and suchlike. You're sitting here hamstrung by instructions about what's allowed and what's not allowed. Guidance from the Red Cross. Am I right?"

She was searching her handbag for lozenges. She held the packet out to me, but I refused; it mentioned something about eucalyptus on the blue-and-white wrapper. Perhaps she was actually nervous after all, and her mouth was dry.

"I've come to listen to what you've got to say," she explained. "To what's on your mind. To what's weighing on your conscience, if you've done something wrong. And if not, I'll listen to your concerns. But not a word, not a syllable of any of this can I pass on. I have a duty of confidentiality. Like a Catholic priest."

She smiled good-naturedly.

"I'd like to think they're treating you well. But there isn't much compassion in a place like this. And a life without compassion is a lonely life. I often think about that."

Her eyes took in the wretched visiting room: worn furniture; a few pictures on the walls; a water sprite rising up from a tarn with green, gleaming eyes; a squirrel in midair, sailing from one branch to another; dirty windows. Then something came to her mind and suddenly she grew eager. She leaned forward in her chair, her eyes shining with a special intensity.

"I bet you can't guess who walked to the park yesterday? I mean, under her own steam. That young girl, you know, the one who always sat in a wheelchair. Do you remember her, and her mother?"

"Miranda," I said with surprise. "Are you seriously telling me she can walk? She can't walk; she's disabled."

Ebba nodded. "She's got braces on her legs. She can't bend her knees, of course, but she is walking. One little step at a time. I nearly fell off my bench; it was like a miracle. I've never seen a child so proud."

"How wonderful," I said halfheartedly.

And I tried to imagine the scene. The thin girl strutting along on stiff legs. And that walking nail display, Lill Anita, following behind with supporting hands. And I didn't like it a bit; I didn't like the way the image I'd formed long ago of the two of them, the mother and the child with all her spasms, suddenly had to be modified now. It was as though I'd lost control of life. Leg braces. Well, really.

"But surely she can't run?" I put in.

"Oh, no, I doubt she'll ever do that. But just imagine the feeling of standing on your own legs at last and being able to walk with your mother to the park. Just imagine it!"

For a while, I sat immersed in my own thoughts. I believed I could glimpse the outline of a pattern that until now had been hidden. And I was a tiny part of this complicated weft, perhaps an insignificant part, like one thread in a net. And Ebba and Miranda were, too; and the big black man from the Reception Center; Lill Anita; and Arnfinn, whom I'd clubbed to death. We were simply minute pawns, and we were being moved around. The notion that some other being had an overarching plan for me and my affairs sent a shiver down my spine—a being I could neither glimpse nor control.

"Can you see the sanatorium from your window?" Ebba asked. "My husband spent a month there as a patient many years ago. Lots of people say it's haunted."

"Yes," I said, "I've heard that. How stupid can you get. As if the dead could be bothered to moon around, once they've finally gotten free of this world."

"It's supposed to be haunted by a former nursing sister," Ebba explained. "At night you can hear creakings from doors and stairways. Witnesses have seen a bluish light in the corridor, something icy cold that stands there flickering; it's quite inexplicable.

But, you know, there's lots of wood in that old building, so it's not surprising that there are noises. The timbers are affected by the weather, and a house is a living organism. And then there's static electricity. Nature is full of forces. Who's looking after your house?" she inquired suddenly.

"No one," I replied. "And I worry about it."

She reached down to find a handkerchief in her bag and sat there with it in her hand.

"Yes, my husband's dead," she announced. "It's fifteen years ago now. He suffered another major embolism only a year after his first one, and we didn't get to the hospital in time. But I'm sorry; I didn't mean to go on about my own affairs. I can help you as regards your house," she said. "We've got a volunteer service, and they take on jobs like that."

I thought of Arnfinn's grave.

"No," I said, "it'll be all right. It won't be long before they give me some leave, and there's not much that needs doing. The lawn's wild anyway, and the house is in good order."

She took another lozenge.

"How do you pass the time? Do the days hang heavy? I imagine the nights must be worst. I mean, the loneliness. And the dark. The worry, all those thoughts. And perhaps an uncertain future."

"I've certainly got quite a lot to think about," I said. "And the ones who've brought this charge will have plenty to think about, too, when they realize they've arrested the wrong man. But I'm certain the truth will come out. I mean, I believe in justice. I have to believe in it, or I wouldn't be able to keep going."

I looked into Ebba's earnest face. She had some lines and wrinkles, slightly pendulous jowls, and her hair was gray: all signs that she'd been around a long time and that the years had set their mark upon her. She sucked eagerly at her lozenge and sat on the edge of her chair, all attention; someone had taught her the art of listening, or perhaps she had a natural gift for it.

"How often can you come?" I asked, feeling as needy as a small child.

"Ah," she said, prevaricating. "I have several people to visit. But possibly every other week if I can manage it. How does that strike you? Every fortnight, Riktor? You needn't feel we have to meet. I'll only come when you want me to, not if you don't. Then we'll see how things go on from there. I'm sure it'll work out."

She crossed one leg over the other, their length showing to advantage.

"Guess what happened yesterday," she blurted out suddenly.

"Go on," I said.

"Some divers found a body at the bottom of Lake Mester. They were amateurs, and it must have given them quite a shock. At first they thought it was a rotten tree trunk. But it turned out to be a man, and he'd been there some time. He'd gone missing at the beginning of April; isn't that terrible? Presumably he'd gone skiing and went through the ice. Then he must have thrashed around in the water, quite alone and helpless. But at least the poor soul will have a grave now. That must be a comfort to the family, don't you think? But he must have been an awful sight. After so many months in the water."

She clasped her hands in her lap. Her two gold rings glowed. Sunlight fell obliquely into the room and found us as we sat, each on our own chair, and slowly we were warmed through and through.

"When does your case come up?" she asked.

"Oh, that could take some time. People often spend several months on remand. Some as much as a year, so it'll be a bit of a wait."

Something else came to her, and she became enthusiastic again.

"D'you recall that elderly chap with the hip flask?" she queried. "Who always sat on the bench drinking?"

"Yes, I remember him well," I answered, in a somewhat subdued tone.

"He's completely disappeared," she said. "And the police have put him on the missing persons' register."

"Oh?" I said. "Missing? Disappeared?"

"It seems he had a daughter who lives and works in Bangkok. She's never had much contact with him, but there's obviously been a few words now and again. Then, suddenly, he wasn't answering the phone. Over a long period. Now she's gone to the police, and they've started looking for him. There was a piece in the paper recently, with a picture too. 'Have you seen this man?' And I had, so many times. He's been staggering around the park all these years, poor man. So I got in touch with the police."

"Did you phone?" I asked inanely.

"Yes, I phoned. You know, with what information I had. That he hung around the park and that sort of thing, just in case they didn't know. You two had a certain amount of contact, didn't you? Wasn't he an acquaintance of yours?"

I almost shot up from my chair.

"No, no!" I countered rapidly. "Most certainly not. We weren't acquainted at all!"

"But I thought I saw the pair of you together a couple of times, over at your house. Did I make a mistake?"

"Yes, that's totally wrong. We never exchanged a word. I mean, I know who he is, but we never had anything to do with one another. I don't know where you got that from! Did you really tell the police that we were acquainted?"

"Oh, do forgive me," she said quickly, assuming a worried expression. She placed a hand in front of her mouth and hung back a good while. "But I'm afraid I also told the police that I saw you together. You live in that red house at Jordahl, don't you? The small house with the covered veranda?"

I nodded dumbly.

"Yes, I've seen you there several times; you sometimes cut the grass in front of your house with a scythe. And I saw Mr. Jagge up there at your house a few times. Can I really have been so wrong?"

"Mr. Jagge?" I queried uncomprehendingly.

"Arnfinn Jagge," she replied. "That's his name. I only mentioned it in passing to the police that he was occasionally at your house at Jordahl. Of course, I didn't know your name, but they knew the house. So it's possible they may contact you, in case you can tell them anything. I'm dreadfully sorry if this causes any difficulties for you. You see, I was so certain."

She tried to settle herself again. But a deep furrow had appeared in her brow.

"Maybe they've been to your house to ask about him," she reasoned, "not realizing you're in here; and the one hand doesn't know what the other's doing. That's what it's like in all government departments. It's so strange when someone suddenly vanishes like that, don't you think? But they'll find him all right. One fine day. Even the man at the bottom of the lake was found eventually. Right tends to triumph in the end," she concluded.

I had no answer to that.

Ebba's news had made me feel faint. As if I didn't have enough on my plate already, what with the case pending, the wrongful case. My finger found a hole in the chair seat, bored its way in, and pulled out a thread that I twiddled with almost frenetic fervor. While I tried to come to terms with the situation. While I did my best to regain control.

"What about your case?" Ebba asked. "Are you very worried about it?"

I assured her that I wasn't. I pulled myself together and sat up, my voice strong and steady.

"I'm innocent, you know," I explained. "And there's something about the truth. It gives one strength."

30

I TOLD MARGARETH about the hidden pattern I believed I'd found in my life, and she listened attentively. She nodded occasionally and agreed. She also felt part of some larger plan and that her life was inching toward a particular end—an end that had been ordained for her alone.

"I simply drift along," she said, "as there's no point in questioning everything. There are so many answers you never get. No, it's just a case of girding yourself up and doing your duty. All this how and why, and what's the real meaning behind everything. I've given up caring about that."

Margareth and I were standing in the gleaming prison kitchen, frying enough meatballs to feed twenty. Margareth made the mixture and I molded the small round balls in my hand and placed them in the browning butter. Immediately there was an angry hissing and a delightful smell.

"But that doesn't mean it's impossible to get away," I heard Margareth say. "We can leave the things that are familiar to us and find a new purpose. When we really have to. Start a new life in a different place. Don't you think so, Riktor?"

She had spoken my name again, and my heart leaped. I stood with a meatball in my hand. The raw mixture was so cold and sticky to the touch that I had to struggle against a sudden urge to throw it across the room and watch it splatter on the opposite wall. And slide slowly down the white tiles toward the floor. These were the kinds of whims that would flash through my head. But I kept calm. I was in the process of developing a degree of self-discipline I'd never mastered before. It was because of the routine and the narrow cell; there wasn't any room to let fly. It was like being firmly contained inside a cylinder.

"You're probably right," I said. "It's quite possible. But today I was talking to a young man who's in jail for the eleventh time. He certainly hasn't managed to get out of the rut. The eleventh time. That only means one thing. He's lost."

"That's a bit cruel," Margareth cut in.

"No, I'm just being a realist," I said.

She wanted to know if I'd met the Russian. She described him as huge and awe-inspiring, completely bald and with a large tattoo on his forehead, which had originally depicted a scorpion; but over the years it had stretched a bit at the edges and now looked more like a great cockroach crawling across his brow. He was in for armed robbery and bullied the other prisoners to such an extent that the management was considering putting him in solitary.

"I've met him in the exercise yard," I replied. "He asked me what I'd done to my teeth. Whether I'd filed them down on purpose or if they'd just gone like that. So I told him they were the teeth I was born with. That's the only contact I've had with the Russian."

"He's been here before as well," said Margareth. "A couple of years ago. He'd robbed a jeweler's shop with three others. Grind a bit more pepper over the meatballs, please. Well, go on, man! The boys like them nice and hot."

I went on and on, grinding pepper over the meatballs. By now I'd become very used to these hours spent in Margareth's company; every day I looked forward to them with pleasure. Margareth, dear Margareth. Those unassuming conversations, the calm and reserve of her personality, her ever-downcast eyes. She was certainly no beauty—no Anna Otterlei—but I'd accustomed myself to the mascaraed eyes and the dry, red hair, which she often concealed beneath a frayed scarf. But all the time I was plagued by one great anxiety. I feared the day her assistant might be passed fit to work again. Then, presumably, I'd be banished from the kitchen and left to my own devices, alone in my cell. The mere thought of losing the treasure that I'd at long last discovered was enough to trouble me. And the fear suffused and disturbed me, especially at night. I slept fitfully and had nightmares about all that had happened, and that which might happen in the future. I'd dream that Arnfinn had risen from his grave, toppled the rhododendron bush, and walked all the way to the prison to denounce me. He'd stand by my bed with a swarm of flies around his head and fat, yellow maggots crawling out of his mouth. I'd never seen such fat maggots. These anxiety attacks also affected me during the day when I was working in the kitchen. They came from nowhere like bolts of lightning. I'd have to lean on the work surface and breathe calmly for a couple of minutes before continuing work. Margareth said nothing. She worked steadily on, as the smell of meatballs with onions and nutmeg filled the kitchen.

31

SOMEONE, I DON'T know who, had slipped into Nelly Friis's room. Had stood there staring at her for a few moments. Maybe sat on the chair by the bed, murderous hands in his lap, thinking evil thoughts. Then this person had risen, pushed back the chair, pulled the pillow from under her head, grasped it firmly, bent over her, and forced it against the thin face with all of his strength. Presumably Nelly's body had gone through some spasms, but she'd probably lost consciousness fairly quickly, debilitated as she was by age and ill health. Then there was silence in Nelly's room. Only one person was left breathing hard after the crime. He'd replaced the pillow beneath her head and crept out. Perhaps this person was on the staff at Løkka. Or a relation, possibly. Relatives came and went as they pleased, and we couldn't always keep tabs on them. Of all the people who worked at that large institution, the police had singled me out. And I didn't know why. I always made my moves with the greatest caution and checked left and right before I entered a room. I pulled hair and pinched and scratched, but no one ever saw me do it. Even so, I'd noticed the atmosphere: their long resentful looks as if they knew something anyway. I couldn't understand it.

. . .

My case was scheduled at last.

It was fixed for November 10. And Margareth's assistant had been diagnosed with bone cancer. Slowly but surely the cells of the disease were eating away at his bones, and in the end he would collapse like a house of cards. What happy news! I reveled in it like a small child. It secured my place in Margareth's kitchen. I employed the four remaining weeks in preparing myself thoroughly, and I admitted to Margareth that I'd find it hard to leave her. That soon I'd be alone again in my own little kitchen, with no one to talk to.

"Well, only if they find you not guilty," she said tersely.

I smiled self-confidently. I didn't believe I would be sentenced for a crime I hadn't committed; after all, we live in a country under the rule of law.

De Reuter organized some decent clothes for me. Nice gray trousers and a navy blue blazer, a shirt and tie. I was respectability itself in this outfit, although it was actually a size too large. Now I experienced the ticking passage of time in a new way, all those hours and minutes, for at last I had an objective. I was on the way to release. I practiced many long speeches I intended to make to the court, delivering them in a firm and steady voice. But de Reuter told me in no uncertain terms that I must obey all the judge's instructions. I promised to do as he said.

"I promise," I would say, my right hand raised, "to tell the truth, the whole truth, and nothing but the truth."

The night before the case was due to be heard, I couldn't sleep. Arnfinn was pressing in so close again that I could smell him. I rose from my bed several times and went to the window and peered out at the sanatorium, and saw that there were lights in several of the windows. I thought of the grave behind my house, and if, by now, wind and weather had leveled it. I imagined it had. I lay down again. I listened to the muffled sounds from outside and thought of the Russian also lying on his bed, his great body and high forehead with its black cockroach. Perhaps the cockroach came alive at night. Perhaps it crawled around his head until dawn and then returned to its usual place on his brow. Then my mind turned to Arnfinn's daughter in Bangkok, the one who'd discovered he was missing. Then to my house at Jordahl, which stood empty. I tossed restlessly in bed. For a long time, I lay against the wall with my knees drawn up. Then I turned onto my back before rolling onto my side once again. I drew the covers over myself and huddled down, all the time mumbling: the truth, the whole truth, and nothing but the truth.

32

FOR ONE MAD moment, I wondered if Margareth mightn't be in court. Her red hair shining lustrously from the rows of blue chairs, a freckled hand raised in a wave. But the idea was idiotic. Margareth was in the kitchen busy with her work. She wasn't concerned about me or hoping for acquittal; she was indifferent to me and my fate. This thought depressed me, hope seeped away, and the judge and jury loomed like a hydra-headed troll.

In the courtroom, there was a large flat screen, about fifty inches wide. For some reason, this screen disturbed me, and my eyes constantly turned toward it. I tried to think what it might be for but finally came to the conclusion that it must be part of the courtroom furniture. For cases where there was visual evidence. Now the preliminaries began. In a loud, clear voice, I pleaded not guilty to the charge of aggravated murder. My eyes were fixed on the elderly judge.

"The indictment is presumptuous, unfounded, and extremely serious," de Reuter said. "My client knows nothing whatsoever about these allegations."

I sat there staring at the black screen. No matter where I let my gaze wander, I was always aware of that dark rectangle on the periphery of my vision. It reminded me of something unpleasant. If

I looked at it for too long, it seemed to draw me in, and I feared I would get sucked into its matte blackness, as if into quicksand.

I remained cool and collected all the time, just as de Reuter had instructed. I sat silently listening to the counsel for the prosecution, looking the judge in the eyes and concentrating on making a good impression. Clandestinely I watched a couple of journalists taking frequent notes and an artist sketching. I watched his pencil work over the paper in rapid strokes.

"I've known Riktor for a little over eleven years," Anna said when, after several hours of evidence from the pathologist and other experts, she entered the witness box.

"He was trained at the National Hospital, and he applied for a job at Løkka in 1999. I conducted the interview. I noticed even then, during the long conversation we had, that there was something a bit odd about him. Well, in a variety of ways. But there aren't that many nurses who want to work in an environment like ours, and particularly not male nurses. So I couldn't afford to be too critical. 'Why are you keen to work with old people?' I asked, prompting him to justify his choice, to show he really wanted to work at Løkka. When he could have worked in an accident and emergency department or as a paramedic: a job with a lot more drama and excitement, the way men often prefer it.

"And I remember his answer. He said, 'Because that's the biggest challenge. That's the greatest drama. People who have nothing but death left. And the things I'm able to give them could be the last things they'll ever get. I like this challenge, this idea, because it makes me very significant. If you give me the job, that is.'

"And I did. Because I thought he made such a good case. And I regret it to this day, my God, how I regret it. In all honesty, I don't think Riktor is quite right in the head. But there are only a few of us who know about it. On the outside, when dealing with most people, I mean, he seems perfectly normal and he's very articulate. But I know that he goes around torturing the patients, and he was especially bad with Nelly Friis. I've known about it for some time, and several of us on the ward got together to catch him red-handed."

Anna paused. She gazed over at me and her look was full of accusation; it was unbearable. I tried to work out what she was driving at. I tried to think about the future, which I'd tentatively begun to plan for myself—something new and better, a new element in my life that could raise me out of the rut. And into the arms of Margareth, once and for all. Away from the shamefulness of my old life, away from the diesel engine that rumbled throughout the night, and the teeming, fly-like buzzing in my head that had plagued me for such a long time.

"Nelly would sometimes start fretting when Riktor entered the room," Sister Anna said.

She stared in my direction once more with recrimination in her eyes.

"At first we couldn't work out the reason. But gradually we began to have terrible doubts; one discovery in particular really filled us with fear. One day I found some tablets in the pan of Nelly's toilet. And that was peculiar because Nelly couldn't move. She never left her bed. More and more of us began to share the suspicion that he was flushing medication down the toilet. And we decided to do something about it once and for all. And so we bought a video camera."

I sat there open-mouthed with fear. There could be no doubt she'd said a video camera. I couldn't take it in; I felt as if I was falling through the floor. The black screen loomed larger, and at last I understood its significance: they had visual evidence. At last I saw that the staff had laid a trap.

And now it snapped shut.

The scarlet of shame spread across my face. At the same moment, I noticed that de Reuter was gasping for air.

"We placed the camera on a shelf," Anna continued, "with the lens pointing toward the head of Nelly's bed. We covered it with a couple of towels and left it there for a good while. Until we'd collected the evidence we needed."

A court usher crossed the floor.

Slow, heavy steps. He put a disc in the DVD player, withdrew, and seated himself again. It was as if everyone in the courtroom had ceased to breathe. An image appeared on the screen, fifty inches wide, and clearly visible to everyone present. The judge and jury could see it, the prosecuting counsel could see it, the press and the court usher could see it. The artist and de Reuter could see it, the prison officers and police could see it, Randers could see it, and the pathologist could see it. I was lost. It was like falling from a vast height, falling in slow motion. We saw a sickroom with a bed and lots of apparatus next to it: a chair; a lamp; and a bedside locker with a plastic beaker on it, indicating the patient had been given something to drink. I recognized the room at once. Because one of her great-grandchildren had done a drawing of a huge red heart and had hung it over her bed.

Nelly Friis lay in the bed. Still, pale, and helpless. For quite a few seconds, the picture didn't alter. Nelly's emaciated face, the red heart on the wall. Then there were footsteps and the barely audible closing of a door. And then a newcomer in the frame. A man in a white coat was bending over the bed. In his hand was a small container with white tablets in it.

My own voice was easily recognizable to everyone present.

I'm not giving you any candy. What d'you want candy for; you're almost a hundred.

Then I vanished from the screen for a few seconds. There was the sound of the toilet flushing. Then I was back by the bed again.

It was as silent as the grave in the courtroom. Silence, as they all watched how I pinched Nelly and tweaked her hair. She started whining and tried to get away, but she couldn't get away. Nor had she the strength to cry out. De Reuter leaned over to me and whispered in my ear.

"You're not making things easy for me. Have you got any other secrets I should know about?"

I had no answer. I hung my head like a whipped dog, while pictures continued to fill the spacious screen.

I instantly recognized the room in the basement, where we placed the dead. The camera had been positioned there, too, and their trap set. Ingemar Larson was lying on the bier, with a white sheet drawn up to his chest. A candle burned on the small table next to it. And, of course, I recognized myself, dancing around in my white coat while pulling the most grotesque faces. I was chanting and gesticulating, as if death were a joyous occasion. I looked like a clown. It was so obvious to me, now that I could actually witness my own behavior, that people found it thoroughly shocking. And that future, which I'd been so determined to build, was running through my fingers like sand. To put it bluntly, I mocked Ingemar Larson shamelessly. And everyone could see me doing it.

I tried to regard what was happening as my confession. That it was essential for staking out a new path, a wholesome path, the one I would travel with Margareth. That it would certainly do some good in the long run, even though it was ghastly now. I thought of this as the witnesses came forward with their tales and their opinions about me and the things I would stoop to. And it was obvious that they assumed that anyone who could pinch and scratch, and cheat people of medicine, could also kill. Now the scales fell from my eyes. They had an agenda.

"I rarely find myself rendered speechless," the judge announced. "But I am now."

Sali Singh entered the witness box.

He was clad in those silk pajamas that Indians wear, but no turban. He'd never used a turban all the time I'd known him. His bluish-black hair was impressive. The light fell obliquely from the tall windows into the courtroom and made it shine like gunmetal.

"I have known Riktor for more than eight years. And I thought I knew him. What I am saying is that it is terrible to be so wrong about a person. Because he has always been pleasant to me. Friendly and concerned. And we have had so many decent times in the kitchen together. But when I am looking at these pictures of him, and understanding what he has been doing, then I just feel like going back to Delhi. Forever. They are so terrible; they make me shiver. Because the Riktor I know is dutiful and precise. He is almost never absent from his job, and he is always ready when someone needs him. He is always in good humor, and he often praises others. He praises my food and he praises Anna and Dr. Fischer when he has the opportunity. But I do not know much about Riktor's private life, I have to say. Things like family and so on, whether he has any. And I do not know what he does in his free time, or whom he is with. I could never bring myself to ask him these private questions. He always keeps a little distance. Then, some rumors started about him, which I dismissed at first as malicious gossip. It was impossible to believe them. But both Anna and Dr. Fischer stuck to them. They thought that he was torturing the patients. And now the court has seen what happened, that he fell right into their trap. With that camera hidden on the shelf. After that, we thought we had enough to report him and get him sacked from Løkka Nursing Home once and for all. We had removed the camera by the time Nelly was killed.

171

It is strange to think that we could have gotten it on film. And his dreadful behavior in the basement, with Ingemar Larson. Such complete contempt for death. I have never seen anything so bad in my life."

"The worst thing about it," Dr. Fischer said, "is when I think back over those eleven years. Of the many patients who've been with us at Løkka during that time. That perhaps he tortured all of them, in some way or other. Perhaps he's killed several people without us discovering it. Perhaps he's been carrying on without our knowledge for all that time, while we've been totally blind to it. I suspect this is the case. And the notion is unbearable. I've puzzled so often over prescriptions that didn't have the intended effect, but now I know why. There's been a lot of uneasiness among the patients, often when Riktor was in the room and close to the bed. But we never managed to put two and two together. We ought to be thoroughly ashamed of ourselves, all of us. But we were never thinking along those lines; we thought of him as able and unflagging. It's terribly unpleasant to be so wrong about a person. It threatens my self-esteem. Because I'm the one in overall charge of the ward."

"I've always thought there was something quite different about him," said Anna. "He's the sort who used to slink around. Suddenly, he'd pop up from nowhere, with that peculiar smile of his, as if he'd been standing there waiting. And there he was, with a touch and a friendly word. But now I see everything in a different light, and it's so horrifying. And when I think of poor old Nelly, lying there gasping for breath, I just feel total despair. For that long, rich, eventful life to be terminated in such a base manner. Sometimes I don't know if I can carry on in the job. It's so hard to go into the room where all this happened. I thought we ought to clear that room, remove the bed and lock the door, and leave it empty forever.

"But life isn't like that. I had no choice; I was forced to wheel in another patient."

33

"I DIDN'T KNOW they were going to place me in a position like that," I said apologetically to de Reuter, when at last we were alone together. He claimed I'd broken my side of the bargain, and asked if I had any more secrets, which I denied.

"We'll have to alter our strategy now," he said, "and tighten up our defense. You're going to need every bit of help you can get. Is there anything else I should know?"

"No. From now on, I'll lay all my cards on the table," I promised. "I know I've said this again and again, but I'm not guilty. I mean, as regards the murder. The other thing is a regrettable problem I've struggled with for many years. But that's over now. Everything's behind me, and I promise to control myself."

He barked a farewell as he headed for his car and drove off.

The prosecution ordered psychiatric tests to find out if I was responsible for my actions. The forensic psychiatrist was an elderly man, a little over sixty perhaps, with hair that resembled a silver lid on the top of his head. He wore glasses with bold frames and thick lenses, a polka-dot bow tie, a suit that was a couple of sizes too large, and stout brown shoes scuffed at the toes. A couple of shiny hairs stuck up from the top of his head and formed a small antenna. I sat there staring at it, fascinated by the two unruly hairs that wouldn't lie down. He had that knowing melancholy typical of psychiatrists, visible as a tint of sadness in his gray eyes.

"Presumably you think I'm suffering from a personality disorder," I began.

We were in one of the prison's meeting rooms. He smiled and smoothed his hair; the tiny antenna prostrated itself neatly. But only for a couple of seconds, then it sprang up again.

"Is that the category you want to belong to?" he asked. His voice was mild and friendly. "Would it make everything that's happened easier to bear? If that was the conclusion I reached?"

I thought for a moment. "It makes no difference. Because I know who I am. But what I don't know is how I got to be the way I am. Don't ask about my childhood," I added. "There's nothing to say about it. Nothing at all."

"So you weren't mistreated in any way, or neglected?"

"No, I was simply overlooked. Perhaps that's almost as bad."

"But was it a difficult time?"

"No, but not very much happened. My childhood was long and uneventful. My father went to work before I got up in the morning, and he returned home long after I'd gone to bed. I hardly ever saw him. He was home on the weekends, of course, but then he was ensconced behind a newspaper. Or sleeping on the sofa. My mother kept house—she was forever washing, or cleaning, or polishing. She didn't say much. She'd answer me if I asked about something, but only quite perfunctorily. They were both very reticent. I did well at school, at least in terms of schoolwork. There's nothing the matter with my head, just in case you're wondering. My schoolmates called me 'The Pike.' And I found that quite difficult. The school dentist announced that he'd never seen teeth like mine before, but we didn't have the money to do anything about them. The first time I sat in the dentist's chair, the dentist shouted to his assistant who was working in the next room: 'Vera! Come and take a look at this! I've never seen teeth like these in all my life.' There, that was my childhood. I don't remember much more than that."

"Well then, let's leave it. We can return to it later. Now I'd like to hear you say something about helplessness. What do you feel when you're faced with a dependent person?"

"Irritation. Resignation. I get angry, and I despise them for clinging to others, for begging and whining and complaining. I'm being totally honest now, and that's no easy matter as I work in one of the caring professions. But now I really want to be understood."

"What about despair? Do you feel that too?"

"After only a second or two, I feel completely inadequate. I've got to do something, and do it right away. I've got to find an outlet for my own frustration. There's a name for that, isn't there?"

"You really do want a diagnosis, don't you," the psychiatrist said. "And perhaps we'll arrive at one before we've finished. But what about you? What if you became ill or incapacitated, or needed help in some way. How would you manage?"

"Pretty badly," I admitted. "I'd despise myself as much as I despise others. I'd go to the dogs. I'd go into a decline and never get up in the morning again; I'd never look at myself in the mirror. Never!"

The psychiatrist had a folder. He opened it now and took out a sheaf of papers.

"What about the videos? What was going through your mind when they were shown to the court? What do you imagine people think of you after that?"

"They're probably disgusted. People can't take very much. But sometimes those of us who work with dementia lose patience. It's not just me, there's a number of us."

"So you're saying that others on the ward might also have tortured the patients?"

"That's obvious. Somebody killed Nelly Friis. Someone who lost patience. Or someone who wanted to take pity on her. I don't know, but it wasn't me. Almost anything could have happened in that room. And in the other rooms. We're only human after all."

The psychiatrist made notes. His antenna waved every time he nodded, two thin streaks of silver.

"I'll tell you one thing," I said. "Nelly Friis's murder will never be solved."

"Why not?"

"The judges have already made up their minds. They've seen the videos."

"It has to be proved," he commented.

"No, I'll be convicted on circumstantial evidence. Randers said so himself. People have been found guilty on circumstantial evidence before."

"So you don't believe in justice?"

"Not after this. But occasionally I glimpse a pattern. And I've often gotten the feeling that people are following me with their eyes and laying traps."

"You feel you fell into a trap?"

"Of course I fell into a trap. I fell into it headlong, and I'm bitter about it. You think what you like, but a hidden camera is pretty low."

"You chose to work with people," the psychiatrist said. "Why did you do that? What was it about the job that attracted you, when you say you've got serious problems dealing with other people's helplessness?"

"Well, I suppose it's death," I admitted.

"What do you mean?"

"I'll be perfectly frank, but please don't jump to any conclusions regarding Nelly. The patients we care for only have death to look forward to. And I like being in the proximity of death."

"Explain that to me," the psychiatrist said.

"It has its own drama. I enjoy it; it excites me. And you must make a note that I'm confiding something important to you."

He noted down what I'd asked, a hint of a smile on his lips. Then he pointed to his papers and tapped the thick bundle with a finger.

"We'll do an interview. It's called an SCID interview, and it'll take about ninety minutes to go through all the questions. The interview will reveal any personality disorder you may be suffering from, and if so, what sort of disorder it is. It's an attempt to chart your most important characteristics. Characteristics that are typical of you, which have existed most of your adult life and aren't confined to periods of particular depression, anxiety, or lack of engagement. Suspicion and confidence, for example, are things we can have more or less of. What we're looking for is how much you differ from a hypothetical average individual. If you answer 'yes' to a question and acknowledge the characteristic, it means that you believe you are more like that than most other people. And you score three points. Let me give you an example. If you answer 'yes' to the question 'Have you had difficulty making decisions by yourself?' that indicates that you think it's been more difficult for you than for most people. D'you follow me?"

I nodded.

"You can score from one to three points on each question," he added. "By the finish, we'll have a classification."

I said I understood, and he began immediately. He asked me about my talents. He asked about my schooling and working life and handicaps. Whether I had close relationships with people, and I had to answer no to that, of course. Apart from Arnfinn, and that hadn't lasted long.

"Do you often worry about being criticized or rejected in social situations?" he asked. "Do you think you're less good, clever, or likeable than most other people? Do you often detect hidden meanings in what people say or do? Do you get angry when you're offended? Do you like being the center of other people's attention? Do the majority of people not appreciate your unique talents and achievements? Do you often think about the power, fame, or recognition that will one day be yours? Do you believe that very few people deserve your time and attention? Do you feel that your own situation is so unique that you are entitled to special treatment? Would you say it's true that only very few things make you happy? Do you have the feeling that there is a person or a force around you, even though you can't see anyone? Last but not least: have you ever had fits of anger so violent that you've lost control?"

Yes. I've lost control all right. Of course I answered yes to every one of these questions, these insinuations. I've had fits of anger and I've lost control. I was exhausted when the interview was over, but I gave him what he wanted. I scored the maximum possible, feeling a kind of strange contentment as I did so. Because now I belonged somewhere, among the disturbed, and my condition had a name. But I didn't mention that I'd once stuck a cannula in Nelly's eye. And punctured a small blood vessel that made her eye bloody and red. This only happened once, and I was simultaneously excited and horrified with myself and my own ingenuity. I didn't mention Margareth either, or what I felt when I saw the beetroot juice on her lips. The madness that inflamed me then, how it began simmering in my trousers. How my pulse beat hard, muffled in my distracted mind.

I said nothing about these.

All evening I sat staring out at the sanatorium. There was no sun, so the windows didn't blaze; the overcast weather made the building seem heavy and gloomy. Janson came in to hear how I'd got on with the psychiatrist.

"He was friendly enough. He asked masses of questions and I answered them all truthfully."

I looked Janson in the eye.

"Tell me something," I asked him. "Have you ever completely lost your temper and done something really terrible?"

Janson, who was his usual lighthearted self, now grew solemn as well. I could see he was searching his memory, examining certain episodes.

"Riktor," he said finally, emphasizing each word. "Everyone loses their head sometimes. Everyone does something terrible. But most things can be put right in one way or another. Almost everything can be put right, if you take the time to do it. But not murder. Murder is irrevocable. Thou shalt not kill," he went on. "You know your Bible, don't you?" He laid a hand on my shoulder; it was heavy and warm. "That's the way our wonderful system works," he said.

"Everyone gets a second chance."

34

THE COURT CASE continued its slow progress, and I went on behaving in an exemplary fashion, despite my serious setback. I still had some of my life before me. It was a question of saving the remnants. But whenever I was back in the prison and entered Margareth's kitchen, I was filled with a huge sense of peace. I'd never felt it so clearly before. To think that one human being could affect another so forcefully—she was as life-giving as the sun, as soothing as spring water. I tried to hold myself in check and was frightened of making a mistake. I was terrified she'd find an excuse to exclude me from the kitchen if I didn't behave. And give the job, which I prized so highly, to another prisoner.

"I suppose you've heard the rumors," I said. "You must have heard people talk about the case and what's come out."

She didn't look at me as she answered. She was browning onions, and now she asked me to take over.

"I've no desire to know anything about that sort of thing," she said in a subdued voice, hurriedly drying her hands on her faded apron. "It's nothing to do with me, and I mind my own business. But somehow, rumors usually reach me in the end. Everyone in here has transgressed in some way or other, so I'm used to it. There. Now you just finish browning those onions. Eight altogether. Sprinkle a tiny bit of sugar on them," she directed. "It gives them such a lovely color. Talking of rumors. Did you know we've got a new one in today? Has Janson told you? From the Refugee Reception Center," she said. "He's from Somalia. They say he attacked one of the staff. He's supposed to be a big man. Larger than the Russian, they say, so you can imagine. He arrived in full combat gear, with leather boots and everything. Apparently he was quite a sight."

My thoughts returned to the park near Lake Mester, and the big black man who had so often come and sat in front of the fountain. Again I perceived the hidden pattern. The sense of being a piece of a larger whole, and that there was a purpose, a grand plan. The huge black man. It had to be him—what a strange coincidence. I sliced an onion until my eyes were streaming with tears, sprinkled sugar over it, and enjoyed the smell that filled the kitchen.

"Open the tap and let it run," Margareth said. "That'll help."

I did as she said.

"Have you got any brothers or sisters?" I asked. I wanted to chat and hoped this would be a safe question to open with. Not something she'd regard as forward or tactless.

She dropped some butter in two large frying pans. And I noticed she was hesitating. I couldn't really see why. Either you've got brothers and sisters, or you haven't.

"I had a brother," she said at last.

"Is he dead?" I asked. "Sorry. It's none of my business; I was just being inquisitive. I'm sorry."

I kept quiet. The butter in the frying pans melted and began to sizzle. It looked as if she were considering, weighing the matter up to herself.

"Yes, I had a brother. He was sixteen," she related. "And he was very good at diving. He taught himself; he never had any lessons. His repertoire included a beautiful, perfect swallow dive that he did from the ten-meter board. All his friends would sit along the edge of the pool and watch, and he used to demand five kroner per dive. He liked that he managed to earn a bit over the summer."

She tightened the apron around her waist.

"But he had another side as well," she continued. "A dark side. Not many people knew about it, but for long periods he'd get very depressed. But then, when we'd begun to feel seriously worried, his spirits would start rising again, and his mind would lighten. And he went on like this, up and down, for several years. My room was next to his. In the evenings, I could hear him playing a lot of gloomy music, and sometimes I'd hear him crying. But I said nothing to the grown-ups. So his life went on like that, a rollercoaster ride. He never had any treatment, and up in the north there wasn't much they could offer people like him, anyway."

She glanced at me and pointed.

"Take that onion out now; it's been done for some time."

I did as she said. I put the onion rings on a plate and started cutting up another. Nice, thin rings, as she'd taught me.

"But those swallow dives of his were famous," she went on. "Have you ever seen a perfect swallow dive?"

I lowered my knife and wiped away a tear.

"Yes," I answered, "but only on television. They are wonderful, you're right. It's the best dive."

"One day he went to the outdoor bathing complex with a crowd of friends. He'd just turned sixteen. They went in a large group and, as he'd so often done before, my brother asked if they wanted to pay to see a swallow dive. As they usually did. And they said they'd willingly pay for a swallow dive. He'd soon amassed twenty-five kroner. When they got to the pool, he took off his clothes and began to climb the ladder to the ten-meter board. His friends sat on the edge of the pool and waited. They said afterward that there was a lot of laughing and joking, nudging and chaffing about what was happening. They cheered and fooled around and called up to my brother at the top of the diving boards: 'You can't chicken out now; we've paid to see it.'"

Margareth poked at the golden-brown beefburgers in the two frying pans.

"He walked to the edge of the board," she said. "And raised his arms. Suddenly everything went quiet, deathly quiet, as one of the boys said afterward when they spoke of what had happened. It was as though a fear had surfaced in them all, a fear that something awful was about to happen. Something they couldn't stop. Because they had pushed him to the edge, in a way."

Margareth straightened her back and put her hands on her hips.

"He waved to them," she continued. "Then he fell forward in a beautiful, wide arc. It was September," she added. "There was no water in the pool."

She turned the beefburgers one by one. Her movements had become quick and clumsy with the thought of what had happened.

"So, perhaps he took leave of life in the spectacular way he'd always dreamed of. In front of a paying audience. He struck head first."

"He really did have a sense of drama," I said cautiously.

"He did," Margareth said. "And my life was never the same again. No sounds from the room next door, no music, no crying. I wanted to die, too, because I had the feeling that he was all alone where he'd gone."

"How old were you?"

"I was twelve. And I remember the funeral as if it were yesterday. We weren't allowed to see him. There was nothing left of his head; it had been smashed to pulp."

She glanced up quickly.

"Well, enough of all this depressing talk. The beefburgers are ready, so you can put them on the plates. And then empty those frozen peas into that pan of water. What about you? Have you got any brothers and sisters?"

"No, nothing," I said. "No parents, no wife, no siblings." I held my breath and steadied myself. Margareth's confidence about her brother had given me courage.

"But I've got you, Margareth," I said.

I thought her cheeks turned a little red just at that moment. And that perhaps her eyes looked shiny. But it was probably just wishful thinking. And anyway, it was very hot in the kitchen.

35

I HARDLY SLEPT a wink that momentous night before judgment was due. The judge would rise and give his verdict: either I was the one who'd pressed the pillow over Nelly's wan face, or there was room for reasonable doubt. Of which I was to have the benefit, naturally; those were the rules. It was a long and exhausting night. The smell of putrefaction in my cell was intense. Time after time, I rose and stood there not knowing what to do, looking around for Arnfinn, and imagining I could hear his hoarse breathing in the nocturnal stillness. Close to panic, I searched my bedclothes for maggots, shook my pillow and duvet, and brushed my hand feverishly over my sheets. I checked the ventilator on the wall, convinced that the smell was coming from there. And I thought I could see a cloudy gas seeping into the room. It settled like a veil around the bed, thick as porridge, filling my nose and head. I couldn't sleep. I lay as if in state, stiff as a board with my arms at my sides, steadfast and immobile.

Around midnight a storm blew up. At first there was just the occasional gust; then it rapidly increased in force. The wind howled around the corners of the big prison building, and after an hour the rain set in with an ominous rush. Its drumming rose and fell as it beat against the walls and windowpanes. I lay on my bed and listened in dismay; the wildness of the elements was so great that night that I imagined it must have some special meaning. A portent of things to come, the verdict, and the disapproval. People turning away in disgust with cold, reproachful looks. Cut off from society once and for all. A reject yet again, a rotten individual. But morning came and the furious wind had abated at last. Immediately I began to think of Margareth and my new life. I told Janson about the foul smell, but he couldn't understand it. He said that no one else had complained and that I was probably just worn out. In that state, we could imagine the weirdest things.

I dressed according to de Reuter's instructions, looking very decent and respectable. Janson accompanied me through the corridors to the back of the courtroom. De Reuter was sitting there with his briefcase on his knees. He seemed bright and alert, not in the least dejected. It was as if he anticipated victory, and that made me nervous.

"Feeling nervous?" he asked affably.

"Yes."

"If they bring you in guilty, we'll appeal. We've got a good case."

It was November 17. The jury members had dressed for the occasion as well, in formal, neutral attire. The indictment had been extended. In addition to Nelly's murder, I was accused of maltreating and persecuting patients at Løkka and obstructing Dr. Fischer's treatment plans, as I had knowingly and willfully sabotaged all medical intervention. I flinched slightly as I sat beside de Reuter. Suddenly, and unexpectedly, I felt a wave of sadness wash over me. Some of it was due to the gravity of the occasion and the fate that might await me. Some was due to Margareth, for she was never out of my thoughts for an instant. It would have been a joy if she'd been present in court. But in a way, it was a relief she wasn't there and couldn't hear the things that were said, the many humiliating conclusions—and there seemed to be plenty of them—about my character and propensities.

The court-appointed psychiatrist had risen and walked to the witness box. He proceeded to explain my disturbed personality. Insensitivity to existing social norms and conventions. A lack of empathy and understanding, a lack of social talent, apathy toward the suffering and misfortunes of others, emotional frigidity, arrogance and sadistic tendencies. Illusions of self-importance and grandeur.

I bowed my head as he listed all my failings, attempting to summon up the requisite degree of humility de Reuter had demanded. The jury spent a long time in reaching agreement, and de Reuter said that was a positive sign. It meant that there was room for doubt. I had to stand to receive their final decision. I clutched de Reuter's arm involuntarily, clutching at hope, silently pleading and praying for justice.

"In the matter of willful murder, we find the defendant not guilty."

I hadn't misheard. The words replayed themselves in my mind: we find the defendant not guilty. I collapsed with relief and, for one brief second, there was room for a merciful God in the emotional chaos within me. That was a new element in my faithless life. And even as I was experiencing this rush, this inexpressibly large release, I received my sentence for maltreatment with head held high. One year's imprisonment, taking into account the time already spent on remand. Two hundred and seventy days left to serve. For harassing and torturing Nelly Friis. For misappropriating Dr. Fischer's prescriptions, and for subjecting dying patients to gross threats. In addition, I was barred from ever working in the caring professions again. But that didn't matter. Margareth, I thought. Justice, I thought; now all I need is to play my cards right.

The press gloried in the details. *Verdens Gang* had its own eye-catching headline the following day.

"The Nurse from Hell."

"Congratulations," said the big Russian.

"Well, I never," said Margareth. And Janson slapped me on the shoulder. Randers had sent me a lingering look in the courtroom as if to say, we're not finished with each other yet, you and I. But we were. And from the moment my cell door slammed shut, I began to serve my time. I gobbled up the days like a famished dog, consumed time with every bit of my energy and ingenuity. I made my own calendar and immediately began a countdown. Now that I'd been given a release date, time passed more quickly. Time had become like a road stretching toward a promised starting post, and this post marked the beginning of a new and honorable life. Janson admired the calendar I'd made. It had 270 small squares, one of which had to be crossed off each evening when the day was over. In the margin, I'd done tiny illustrations for each month. A leafless tree for November, a heart for December, a six-pointed snow crystal for January.

"You can draw," he concluded. "You really can. I'll get you some things, so you can keep working at it."

And so I began to draw each day after dinner; it was a hidden talent I never knew I had. Once I'd started I was unstoppable. I drew the familiar sanatorium and the six-meter-high prison wall with its nests of barbed wire. I drew the exercise yard: the bench, the fence, and the façade of the building with its many windows. I drew Janson as he leaned against the wall with his muscular arms folded. I drew my hand, my foot, my diminutive cell, the bed and the desk. The strokes got more deft and rapid with each passing day. They emanated from somewhere deep within me. They were transmitted through my arm to my hand and flew lightly, even lovingly, over the paper. I liked the smell of graphite when I sharpened the pencil. I lost myself in my drawings. I made up my mind to be a model prisoner, a good example to the other inmates, and called on all my reserves of generosity and discipline. I spoke to the priest, even though I wasn't a believer; it was a matter of making the most of every new impression. I sat in the library and read. Even this was an exercise of sorts, sitting still, concentrating, absorbing. A fortnight after I'd received my sentence, Ebba came to visit. She seated herself comfortably on the chair and immediately took out her crocheting because I'd asked her to bring it along. I enjoyed watching her peaceful occupation.

Her needle moved like lightning. I sat and watched it for a long time.

"Nelly Friis's murder remains unsolved," I said.

She gave me a quick look. Her curls were crisp and newly done; her hair sat like a well-fitting cap.

"That's a problem for the police. They'll work it out all right."

I asked about little Miranda's progress.

"They go to the Dixie," Ebba said, "she and her mother. With their coffee and Coke. Almost every day. What a blessing it is, everything that's happened. She's walking almost normally, but it's taken a long time. When she's wearing baggy trousers, you simply don't know the braces are there. But she can't run, of course. She'll have to plod her way slowly through life. And perhaps that's not a bad thing; you get more out of it that way."

She held her crocheting up to the light and examined her work. I admired the complicated pattern of stars within borders and the minuscule, barely visible stitches.

"You've adapted," she noted. "You're flexible. That's good.

What are you going to do when you're released? It'll be midsummer. You'll need a job."

"They help with that," I explained. "We've got a kind of support service here in prison. But I'm not working with people anymore. It just exasperates me. I can't take people who plead. I can't take people who whine and complain. So I'll have to keep away from them."

"There's good in everyone," Ebba maintained.

I didn't try to deny it. I presented her with a drawing of the sanatorium, in which every one of its windows was an eye looking out on the world. For a brief moment, I toyed with the idea of telling her about Margareth but decided not to. Secrets are my strong point; I wanted to keep it to myself. Our relationship was a bastion for the future, and I added to it, stone by stone, with diligence and care. Margareth knew nothing about it; she didn't know what I was working up to and hoping for. She didn't know about the dream that I was determined to turn into reality. But one day she would see it. She would see the lovely palace and clap her hands in delight.

And so the days and weeks passed. I conformed; I waited. I'd get out and find a job, and then I'd woo Margareth as a free man. With an income and good prospects. With an exemplary record, and my eyes firmly fixed on a new and respectable path. That was the plan.

Humility. Patience. Contrition.

Margareth's assistant passed away.

I dropped my knife in the sink when she told me and almost whooped for joy. I'd never have believed a dead kitchen assistant would have given me so much pleasure. I could have leaped and danced with delight. I could have sprayed a bottle of champagne.

Thank you, O Lord; her assistant is dead! But I stopped myself. After several months in prison, I'd developed a certain amount of tact and propriety. They were the things I needed to conquer Margareth.

When the time was ripe.

Winter arrived and held everything in its icy grip, and the mercury sank toward minus twenty. I feared that the pipes in my house would freeze and later burst, causing leaks in the spring and then damp problems, as well as bills I wouldn't be able to pay. So I was given leave to go and switch on the heating. Of course I thought of Arnfinn lying under his rhododendron bush. Everything was covered in a blanket of snow, even that chapter of my life. I considered that the long year I had to spend alone in my cell would be sufficient punishment for it all. Of course I wasn't perfect. But I felt that I'd have paid for my sins at last.

The asylum seeker from Somalia had become pals with the big Russian, and they made quite a pair as they sat together in the common room. Two great hunks of brawn and sinew. Now, at least, he'd found his niche and no longer had to spend his days playing table tennis. Instead, he went to the gym and got even bigger and stronger, if that was possible. His physique was so muscular that he seemed about to explode. He didn't recognize me. We'd bump into each other occasionally, in the corridor or in the common room, but he looked right through me, his expression vacant. And then, very cautiously, I began to flirt with Margareth. I had to, because time was running out. If I wanted to win her, I'd have to act. Soon she'd understand my motives and realize they were good. All through the winter they were good.

36

NOW THINGS ARE gathering pace.

My release is getting nearer, and the time is ticking toward a new life. To date, Nelly Friis's murder remains unsolved, and I search my mind for a possible explanation. For who's responsible for making a fool of me. For who has committed a crime and then conveniently framed me for it. Because that's clearly what's happened. But perhaps this isn't even a murder. Perhaps the prosecution service is wrong and she died of natural causes, with nothing more than a sigh, and then it was all over.

Blindly and painfully over.

There are various reasons why people can have blood leakage in an eye; I, who stuck a cannula into one, know that only too well. It's no proof of suffocation as the doctor maintains.

I think a lot about Sister Anna, my delightful swan, Anna. And whether she's hoodwinking us. What if her good nature is a camouflage for something else—something that has been going on for years. Maybe several patients at Løkka have been dispatched. I'm not stupid. If I've pulled the wool over other people's eyes, they can do the same to me. I know that Nelly had money. Property, shares, and personal wealth. What if one of the grandchildren, a nephew, a son or daughter, got tired of waiting for the big prize? The final word has not yet been spoken in Nelly's case. But

I know it will be one day. The truth is an unstoppable force; it will come out.

I'm promoted to block monitor.

On account of my exemplary behavior, because now I've learned. I wash the floor of the corridor in front of the cells and hand out the mail. Keep the bulletin board announcements tidy. Pass on messages and take care of small repairs, help shelve books in the library, go on errands from cell to cell, liaise between the prisoners and the prison staff. In short, I'm useful. All day long I help others. I work in the kitchen. I bind Margareth to me with every ounce of zeal and intensity I possess, and I really think she is predisposed toward me. Wasn't opening up about that brother who dived to his death a vote of confidence? Intimate, almost affectionate—that's the way I choose to view it. A green light, so I can advance. Perhaps she's waiting even now. She wouldn't have told just anyone; she chose me. There's no doubt in my soul. Margareth is within reach, and I'm as excited as a child when I think of all that's in store. All that will be mine.

Just as soon as this winter, this long winter, is over.

Just as soon as I've made amends.

The snow melts and runs away.

It gurgles gray and dirty down the drains, taking with it leaves and mud, and scouring the roads clean and smooth. And now everything is easier.

January, February, and March come and go.

And so the months pass slowly by.

Easter arrives, the place on my calendar where I've sketched a chick in the margin. The spring months with all their trickling water and early summer with its shoots. Thus I atone for the hurt and injury I've done the patients at Løkka; I pay the price for my frustrated nature. My lack of control. But I don't complain. Never once have I complained during the long, cold winter. Eventually the snow melts. Summer comes at last, and I'm going to be free again. During the whole of this never-ending year, I've been consummate in all my behavior, and he who has paid the price has surely regained his credit. At least that's my opinion.

I thank Janson for his encouragement and Ebba for the many good times. I walk quietly out of my cell and look over my shoulder at the sanatorium.

I take my clumsy farewells.

The Russian wishes me luck. Margareth doesn't seem particularly affected, but I know her well enough to guess the reason. She's just shy. I manage to stammer something about wanting to stay in contact. She doesn't react to this either but thanks me for my help throughout the year in her dour, bashful way. Janson, too, wishes me luck. "Watch yourself, now," he says. "I don't want to see you in here again. Get a drawing pad and pencil, and get a proper life!" I present him with all my drawings, a thick wad of them. I walk slowly out through the prison gate. Down the road and over to the bus stop. I don't turn to look back because now I'm free. I take a seat on the bus and lean my head against the window. I can feel the engine's vibration through the glass. The droning at my temple reminds me of swarming insects. Familiar, but new all the same. I'm used to my teeming head; I'm sensitive by nature. Now the day has arrived, and the hour, when I'm to begin a new chapter, and I ought to succeed. I enjoy the long bus ride through the streets: the driver's solid presence; the reassuring hum of the engine; and a scattering of raindrops on the window, like mournful tears.

I get off the bus at the Dixie Café because I want to do the last bit on foot. I hesitate as I pass the door of the café, with its two plastic palms in blue pots. It's a pathetic sight, all things considered. Why doesn't someone mention that the décor in front of the premises is cheap and ridiculous? I have a sudden whim and give in to it. I go up to the door, open it, and peer inside. And there they are, the two of them, in the far corner. Miranda and Lill Anita, each with a Coke. Miranda's hair is loose and reaches to her shoulders. No hairbands, no brightly colored plastic clips. She's gotten older. She's wearing trousers with roomy legs. You can't see the leg braces, but I sense their presence because I know they're there. Her legs are stretched out under the table. I retreat before they catch sight of me, and I stroll on.

I return to my house. I stand for a moment in the driveway taking everything in, the cherished and the familiar — all that's mine. I hear my neighbor's children shouting and screeching; they're on the trampoline. Then I take a quick look around the back of the house to see the grave. The rhododendron bush has grown enormous. It's benefited from the sun and rain and is really impressive now. I regard it as a good omen. But one thing troubles me. A narrow path has been trodden from the front steps around to the grave, as if someone has been walking to and fro, checking the terrain. I can't understand it. Perhaps fate is playing a trick on me. Perhaps there's a badger around, or a feral cat. But the path is obvious. A telltale little track from the steps to the grave. A narrow, paler outline in the grass. I dragged a corpse along here. It was heavy. But now that's behind me forever. I let myself in, walk to the window, and look out on the road. I switch on the coffee machine, see the small red light illuminate, hear the water grumble as it heats up, smell the aroma of newly filtered coffee. I have a large cupful and phone the owner of the Shell service station, where the prison has found me work. He's terse and brusque and rather sullen, but I don't have to like him. I like hardly anyone, except Margareth. And Janson. And Anna Otterlei, even though she lured me into a trap. I tell him that I can start whenever he wants; I'm as free as a bird.

We agree on the following Monday. He knows something of my history but was chiefly concerned that my sentence didn't have anything to do with a financial misdemeanor. Once reassured on that point, he felt satisfied and offered me a job on the till at the service station. I'm perfectly happy about this. I'll have to deal with people all day long, but only on a superficial level: only "yes please" and "there you are" and "see you again." No whining, no cares, no carping or complaining. Just fleeting nods and quick smiles across the counter. I'll be serving freshly baked items plus hot dogs, and taking the money for newspapers and gas. Now I can only think about one thing. My first payday. As soon as it arrives, I'll call up the prison and ask for Margareth. I'll finally find the courage to ask her out.

Three days of freedom.

Reading the death notices in the paper, I see that Barbro Zanussi has finally died. It says that she passed away peacefully, but I have my doubts on that score. No one talks about the unpleasant aspects. The rattling and gasping, the disgusting metallic smell from deep within the lungs as they empty for the last time. But at least now she's at peace. The pain and despair are over, and I almost feel relieved for her.

Poor, unfortunate Barbro. Myriad emotions well up and, for a brief moment, I'm filled with compassion. It's dreadful that things can turn out so badly, that life can be so unbearable.

I like reading death notices. I relish them like I would a piece of candy. And Barbro's relatives have chosen a moving poem.

All is bestowed on mankind
Merely as a loan.

All that's mine is owed, soon to be withdrawn again.
For everything is subject to reclaim:
The trees, the clouds, the earth on which I pace.
And then I'll wander lonely, without trace.

I start my new job and manage really well. I'm not especially friendly, but then I don't have to be. I do my job and no one complains. People come in and out; it's a busy place. One day, Eddie and Janne come into the shop, hand in hand, as if conjoined like Siamese twins. Inseparable from the waist down. They look just as happy as ever, and this surprises me greatly. Because I'd imagined that, like Romeo and Juliet, they'd suffer some terrible death in each other's arms. I'd thought that Janne would find another man sooner or later, better looking, stronger. And that Eddie would kill her with his bare hands. Throttle her with a vise-like grip and crush her larynx. Only to take his own miserable life afterward, because things like that do happen. But I seem to have been wrong. They're still together, and they buy a bag of buns. Then they wander out into the sunshine again, ensconced in their bubble of contentment.

It really worries me the way things are going so well for them. Because I can't understand what they've found, that I've never found. But I'm working on it, and I'm moving in the right direction. I count the days just as I did when I was inside; I'm counting down to payday. August is glorious in all its verdant beauty. One day I go to the park by Lake Mester. An unknown woman has taken my bench and, for an instant, I'm indignant. She obviously doesn't know the rules, and she makes no attempt to move when I arrive. She sits rocking a buggy. She's about my own age, probably a grandmother, I think. I find another seat. I perch on the bench that Arnfinn always used. It's good to sit here again, by the fountain. I sit for an hour listening to the tinkling water.

The dolphins are so familiar, so smooth and lithe and wet. On my way home, I stop by *Woman Weeping*. I place my hand on one of the rounded breasts and think about Margareth. Margareth occupies my thoughts entirely; everything else is blotted out by these dreams and the castle that I've built in my mind. I go back to the house. I putter around, gradually adjusting to my new existence as a free man, working for Shell with a regular wage and pleasant coworkers. They know nothing about why I was in prison. In fact, they don't seem very interested in me anyway, and I feel relieved about that. I can hardly expect everyone to see what's unusual about me.

To realize that I'm wholly exceptional.

At last it's silent in my bedroom at night.

There's no chugging diesel engine, no one whispering from the corners of the room.

Ten days of freedom.

Free in the morning, free at midday, and still free in the evening.

One day I make the trip to the cemetery.

I imagine that Anna's brother is likely to be buried here, by Jordahl church. As I begin to work my way through the cemetery, I realize it's going to be hard to find him. The cemetery is large. I wander among the gravestones, reading the odd inscription, halting occasionally to look around me. I catch sight of a man. Presumably he's a cemetery worker, as he's clipping away at a hedge. The clean snap of his shears, with its even and persistent rhythm, is carried on the still air. I hesitate but decide to approach him. He starts when I enter his field of vision; he must have been immersed in his own thoughts. He's wearing a blue cap with a visor and a Honda logo on it.

"I'm searching for a grave," I say. "It's rather important that I find it, but I've no idea where to look. Would you happen to know your way around here?"

"Searching for a grave?" He gives an unenthusiastic toss of his head, as if I've disturbed him in something important. Presumably I have. "Well, it's not easy to say," he adds curtly and lifts the shears again. The sun catches the metal blades. He's both reluctant and ill at ease, but I'm on an important mission so I don't give up.

"He went through the ice on Lake Mester," I explain. "Last year. April it was. Took them forever to retrieve his body; it was found by some amateur divers, almost by pure luck. His name was Oscar. It was an important case, in all the papers. Help me!" I suddenly implore, beseeching him like a child.

He lifts his shears and clips a few twigs. He pushes his cap back on his head; the weather's hot and sweat glistens on his hairline. A few dark hairs stick to his skin.

"Oscar," he repeats. "Yes, I remember the case. A skier, wasn't he? I remember his grave, too; it's a lavish affair. Yes, I know it. There were three hundred people in the church; many more had to stand outside. Go down to the stone wall over there and look in the farthest row."

He points with a bronzed hand. I look in the direction indicated. I thank him and start walking. By the stone wall, in the farthest row, the man who fought and lost. And here am I, the sole witness. I feel a kind of importance as I walk along the gravel path between the gravestones. All these dead people. All these silent souls. And only a few of them are granted the privilege of being ghosts, like the sister at the sanatorium. I want to be a ghost too, I think, as I slowly cross the cemetery. I want to stand there and rumble like a diesel engine. I want to whisper in corners. Then, at last, I pull myself together. I remember that I've changed, that I've served my time. That from now on, my motives will be good. I move on among the graves, until I arrive at the black stone with its gold lettering. The one belonging to Anna's brother Oscar. Died at the age of fifty-three. The gravestone has a nice inscription.

We love you. We miss you.

I kneel and peer over my shoulder at the cemetery worker trimming the hedge. He's not looking in my direction; he's busy with his own affairs.

Then I whisper to the stone.

"There was nothing I could do."

And again, a bit louder.

"There was nothing I could do!"

Someone, perhaps Anna or Oscar's wife, has planted some pansies. The bed is neat and has been lovingly weeded.

Whenever I think about my own death, I'm always worried that nobody will come and tend my grave. But now I've found Margareth. Obviously she'll come, I think, regularly and often. Margareth is thorough and conscientious; she won't skimp. I'd like pansies, too. Such beautiful, velvety flowers with their yellow stamens. I also want to leave voices behind, voices of people who knew me. Riktor, they'll say, we knew him well. Riktor, an old friend of mine. Riktor, my husband. My partner, my best friend. I want what others have got, and I'm going to get it. It's my turn now. Everything comes to those who wait, and I've hesitated long enough. Now I'm going to take life with both hands. It's high time.

I kneel in front of the grave until the small of my back begins to ache.

There was nothing I could do.

I've nothing more to say to Oscar. His recklessness put me in a very awkward position. I can hear the snipping of the shears from the hedge. Then I get up and go. I pass the cemetery worker and nod to him, and walk toward the gate. Now this, too, is a closed chapter of my life.

37

THEN ONE OF the bad days dawns.

But I don't realize it yet, standing by the window and looking out at this known and familiar sight—this little kingdom of mine. The meadowy grass in front of the house and the birch at the bottom of the driveway; it's all mine.

Twenty days of freedom. Two days to payday. The longing for Margareth is like an ache in my body: her hands, her freckles, her mascaraed eyes. It's a new, strange sensation, something I've never felt before.

I think about buying a bunch of flowers and giving them to her on our first date. Making myself as attractive as I can, being generous and gallant; because I'm pretty certain I can be, if I only try. Making an impression on Margareth isn't easy; she's reticent and reserved. But I shan't give up. I'm extremely purposeful. I turn these things over in my mind and make plans, as I gaze through the window. The birch by the road stirs. Then, suddenly, I make up my mind to phone. I decide it's now or never; the impulse strikes me in a flash and I act fast. I pick up the telephone and dial directory assistance, and they give me the number of the county jail. I note the eight digits on a pad, dial the switchboard number, and wait. I can hear it ringing and my heart pounds. The blood roars as it forces its way through my arteries.

Hi, I'll say, when they finally put me through to Margareth. Hi, this is Riktor here. This might be a bit of a surprise, but I want to ask you out.

And if you say no, I'm going to lose my head.

Just then, I see something outside the window — something that gives me a jolt. A green Volvo has turned in, and I start when I see Randers at the wheel. I slam down the phone before anyone can answer and rush out to intercept him at the door. He's standing on the bottom step, as macho and self-assured as ever. The sun bounces off the hood of his car.

"You're a free man, and here I am disturbing you," he says, smiling. "But I won't trouble you unnecessarily, I promise. I only want to tell you something. Something you may be interested to hear, perhaps even have a right to hear. After all that's happened and all you've been through."

I stand in the open doorway and wait. I try to remain calm, but it's not easy. Because once again I'm assailed by a sudden doubt, as if there's still something I've forgotten or overlooked.

"Barbro Zanussi is dead," Randers says. "She was a patient at Løkka, on your ward, wasn't she?"

"I know about it," I say. "Yes, I saw the notice. But I refuse to believe she went peacefully. She probably died with a scream on her lips; she was in great pain."

Randers strolls across the gravel to the side of the house, and I follow.

"There were certain irregularities about her death," he says.

"What do you mean, 'irregularities'?"

"Certain findings that may indicate she was suffocated. Just like Nelly Friis. With a pillow, presumably. And yes, maybe she did scream, as you suggest."

I breathe a sigh of relief, animated by the thought that Barbro had probably been killed in the same way as Nelly. The ultimate proof of my own innocence.

He keeps walking and stops as he reaches the back garden. I want to stop him, but I'm desperate to hear what he has to say.

"Would an apology be in order?" Randers asks.

"Thank you," I say in a measured tone. "Perhaps you ought to have a word with Dr. Fischer. He's the one who always seems to find them. The one who always informs us. I've thought about that a lot."

Randers nods.

"We were about to do that," he says. "But we got there too late."

"How so?" I ask in disbelief.

"Dr. Fischer is dead," Randers says. "He took an overdose. He was terminally ill, in fact. He had a malignant brain tumor. Just here," says Randers, placing his finger on his left temple. "He left a letter. He couldn't bear the thought of life in a nursing home. He knew too much about it. And not to put too fine a point on it, so do you."

I refrain from replying.

"'I am a despicable doctor,' he wrote in his letter. 'And my conscience is heavy.' What d'you think he meant by that?"

"I always knew he'd die of a bad conscience," I say.

"Well, that was all I came to say," Randers remarks.

"I see," I reply, relieved.

"Except for one parting question. We've reopened an old case. A disappearance."

I stand with my hands in my pockets. I feel my nerves beginning to tauten.

"Arnfinn Jagge," Randers says. "He hasn't been seen for a year. You knew him, didn't you?"

"I don't know anyone called Jagge," I answer evasively. "I don't have a lot to do with people," I add. "It's too difficult for me. You know perfectly well that I've got a serious personality disorder."

"So he's never visited this house?"

"No, he's never been here. Never. You won't find anything linking him to me. Or to this place."

"He was an alcoholic," Randers explains.

"Well, in that case, I certainly didn't know him. I don't let just anybody in through the door."

"His daughter has arrived from Bangkok," Randers continues. "She had a business over there for many years, but now she's wound it up and come home. And naturally she wants to discover what became of her father. She's moved into his house. She came to my office yesterday, and I reopened the case to see if we had anything to go on. He was seen here at this house on several occasions. An extremely reliable witness phoned in and tipped us off. So I thought I'd ask you if you had any theories about what might have happened."

"There's never been anyone here called Jagge," I say sullenly.

Randers begins ambling around the garden. I watch him like a hawk. I don't like his self-assured air. He's like a leech. Why can't he just leave, I think. But he doesn't leave; he hesitates. He turns and gazes toward the forest. Perhaps he notices the path. God knows what he's thinking.

"He could have committed suicide, of course. In which case there's nothing to investigate. Perhaps he went into the forest to die. Like an old cat. But, in that case, he'd have been found. Suicides often position themselves where they're easily visible, you know, on a path or close to a hiking trail. And we haven't found him in the forest."

Randers takes a few more steps toward the forest. He halts two or three meters from Arnfinn's grave. I hold my breath.

"That's a fine rhododendron you've got," he says, and walks right up to it. Bends down, holds a leaf between his thumb and forefinger.

"What sort of fertilizer do you use? I have one myself. It's nowhere near as healthy as this. They flower in May, don't they? It must have been quite a sight. But you were still inside then, so you'll have that to look forward to."

"It took care of itself," I say. "It's best to let nature do the work. Don't interfere too much."

He nods and agrees. He stands for a long time at the small mound; it's as if something is holding him back, drawing him to the spot. He gives me a lingering look.

"I'm not usually wrong. I've been in the force a long time. I can smell a crime a long way off. Do you believe in reincarnation, Riktor? I do. Just as a bit of fun. I think we've had other lives. I must have been a bloodhound in one of my previous existences."

I make no answer to this. Because now the miracle happens. Randers turns on his heel and begins to walk toward the house. He turns from the big rhododendron, walks away from Arnfinn's grave, and over toward the green Volvo to drive away.

"But just occasionally even I get it wrong," he says with a smile. Now he's affability itself. Generous and appeasing.

There is justice, I think, and almost feel like whooping. At that moment, he halts in the long grass. On that inexplicable path between the steps and the grave, the path that seems to have made itself. His foot has struck an object in the grass; I hear the hollow sound of his shoe striking metal. He bends and picks something up and cradles it in his hand. And even though it's discolored and tarnished, the engraving is still legible. I realize with a shudder that he's found Arnfinn's hip flask.

38

THEY UNEARTH THE body quickly enough with the aid of dogs.

The rhododendron bush is torn up by the roots, and they work down to the rotting corpse: a thin, hollow Arnfinn, gray and brown, with black hands and feet. He's not a pretty sight. I explain about Arnfinn's gross deceit. Randers isn't interested.

"Talk to your lawyer," he says. "You'll have your day in court."

They put me on remand. I have my photograph and finger-prints taken, and my effects are removed, my wallet and keys. I'm led to an unfamiliar cell and rush to the window to look out. But all I see is a squalid backyard. A dirty, untidy square of junk and garbage. The sanatorium is nowhere in sight, that beautiful building I so often used to rest my eyes on. I sit waiting for de Reuter. In the meantime, a prison officer appears at the door. He's young, unsavory, and rather brash and has pimples around his mouth. I ask him when Janson is due on duty.

"There's no Janson working here," he says, and chews on the gum in his mouth. It's pink and shows itself each time he opens his mouth. His words fill me with alarm.

"What did you say? Doesn't Janson work here anymore?"

He leans lazily against the door frame. Brushes a dewdrop from his nose with his hand and grins.

"We sometimes change blocks," he tells me. "You know, a change is as good as a rest and all that. Your Janson is probably over on B Block; these things happen. Your lawyer will be here in an hour," he adds and leaves. The door slams shut and the lock turns.

I seat myself by the window and stare down into the backyard. At long rows of bins, a rusty woman's bike without a seat, an old shed with a corrugated-iron roof. And there, suddenly I see it: a plump rat scurrying around, looking for food. I have eyes only for the disgusting creature. The naked tail, the shiny coat. And I think of what Ebba once said. A rat in a maze. And you simply can't see over the walls. No trees, no hillsides or uplands, no sun, no blue sky. I try to cling to one comforting thought. Despite all the awful things that have happened, I'm here with Margareth again.

Eventually my counsel arrives at the door.

He's a podgy, bald man. I've never seen anything so sad. Pale, pink, and sweaty. A doughy middle-aged man. Unconcerned and apathetic, little more than a joke as he stands looking in.

"Isn't de Reuter coming?" I ask in exasperation.

The man now scrutinizing me seems both dull and perplexed, not lively and alert like de Reuter.

"I'll be managing your case," he says. "My name is Blix."

He offers me a fat hand to shake. It's cold and limp. He sits down and opens his briefcase; it's grubby and made of artificial leather.

"The police will presumably go for willful murder," he remarks. "The danger is that the prosecution will apply for preventative custody. I see you've got previous form," he adds, looking up at me with an indolent expression. He really is slow, possibly in his mid-fifties, and his breathing is labored. Perhaps he suffers from emphysema or asthma. I try to pull myself together but feel that I'm starting to disintegrate. Those damn flies are starting to buzz in my head.

"A friend abused your trust," he says. "We must use that for all it's worth."

I nod mechanically. I can't believe this is happening. I can't believe this sluggish, flabby man will save my skin; it's not possible. Blix stays for an hour. When he's about to leave, I ask for the officer with the pimples.

"Well, I'll ask him to come. But you'll have to be patient. In prison you've got to wait for everything; you'd do well to realize that right away."

The pimply officer turns up after an unconscionable time. He glowers at me from the door, apathy personified. I explain that I want to send a message. He shakes his head slowly and leans heavily against the sturdy metal door.

"To Margareth," I explain. "She works in the kitchen. Will you tell her I'm back? Will you say it's from Riktor?"

"There's no Margareth in the kitchen," he replies. "Otto works down there. Otto and his assistant, Sharif."

This crushes me.

"You're saying that Margareth's gone? But where is she?" I stammer.

"You mean the one with the red hair? She went up north. Seems to have landed a job somewhere up there, in a nursing home. Northerners, you know what they're like. Always longing for home. They must have a thing about the wind and the sea. Takes all sorts."

Everything I've painstakingly put together simply disintegrates. The castle I've built for Margareth collapses into dust. I look at the young prison officer, and then I lose all control of myself.

I fly at him with every bit of strength I've got, force him against the wall, spit and shout and slobber. I know it will end in solitary, but I can't stop myself.

"I'm going to kill you," I scream. "I'm going to smash your skull and watch your brains run out!"

The door thuds shut. Nothing more. I sit alone in my cell and wait. I stare down at the ugly backyard and search desperately for the pattern I thought I'd discovered, the overarching purpose. That there was some meaning to me and my life. But everything is slowly evaporating, and I congeal in that attitude by the window. An elbow on the table, a hand beneath my chin. A lifeless eye absorbing the ugliness.

I sit waiting for the rat, perhaps it will return; after all, it's something to look at, something alive. Everything has been taken from me. Janson, de Reuter, and Margareth. Instead I've got a rat. At night, after darkness has fallen, I'm still sitting by the window. And the rat does return. A quivering orange rodent in among the bins. I search my mind for something comforting; it's not easy. The time will pass. The hours, the days, the years. I'm on remand, and I'll appear in court. I'll be convicted and have to serve time for old Arnfinn's murder. But sooner or later I'll be out again because that's the way our wonderful system works. Everyone gets another chance, and I'll be out in society once more.

With my disturbed mind, my dark thoughts, and my heart of stone.